AGENT ALONE

REGION TWO SERIES BOOK .5

A PARANORMAL URBAN FANTASY ROMANCE

JANET WALDEN-WEST

JANET WALDEN-WEST

This is a work of fiction. Names, characters, places, and incidents are either products of the author's imagination or used fictitiously, and any resemblance to actual persons, living or dead, business establishments, events, or locales, is entirely coincidental and not intended by the author.

Agent Alone

Region Two Series, Book .5

Contact Information: janetwaldenwest@gmail.com

Cover Art: Black Bird Book Covers jesireland.com

Editor: Jenny Lane Editing

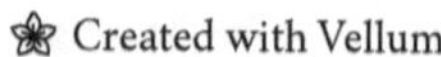 Created with Vellum

CHAPTER 1

idge

MACHETE A FAMILIAR WEIGHT in his hand, Ridge narrowed his focus to the basics. *Eliminate the cryptid. Keep his cadets alive.*

He held his position on the monument base, the bronzed arm of the military hero shielding him and giving him the height advantage. He kept one eye out for their quarry, the cryptid species that'd earned the *ghoul* nickname. The other eye was on the team of cadets better hidden among palm fronds and plantings on either side of the statue.

Sand crunched yards in front of them, Galveston's defining feature betraying the presence of the creature prowling the civilian library's grounds. As the breeze shifted and brought the pong of carrion to him, he revised his mental statement—the cryptic was aiming straight for him and his charges.

This was half mission and half graduation exercise so

they also had the backing of one of the best teams in South-west Region.

But *exercise* really meant an unscripted encounter with a vicious, unpredictable animal. Cryptids might be natural creatures with unnatural abilities, but most were also threats to humanity. And it was their duty to protect the public from them, at all costs.

Hopefully not at the cost of any of the kids he'd trained. After two years of watching them mature, and watching over them, they felt like his kid brothers and sisters.

Company soldiers, not kids. They were the same age he'd been when he completed his graduation requirements. The internal reminder didn't do much to alleviate his worry.

He might've wished for something less vicious than a ghoul, the things his old instructors referred to as Great Whites on legs. Unfortunately, Galveston had lit up with an influx, so ghouls it was as their exercise.

The cadet team would have to handle apex crypto's once they were assigned to their own co-Region anyway. Ridge still strained his hearing to the limits, and still kept part of his focus on the four cadets around him.

The sandy crunch came again, closer and from the left.

Steady. He tapped the code on his earpiece, ghoul senses too keen to use even whispered vocal commands.

For a second, he missed the feel of his sniper rifle, like he'd miss a lost appendage. Instructors weren't to interfere, unless the cadets' performance was so poor it risked allowing the creature to escape. Or cadets were gravely wounded. Stepping in meant the cadet team failed to graduate, but he'd make that call and endure the kids' disappointment before he'd let one die by a ghoul's clawed hand.

The kind of *skree* that heralded doom in horror movies pierced the evening air. Marking claws dragged along iron stair railing. The ghoul had scented them. The noise repeated along with a muffled clank, the creature leaving the flights of concrete steps in favor of the pipe railing.

Playing with them.

He bit down on the warning burning his tongue. The cadets had eighteen years of classes and training. Part of this exam was proving they could read cryptid behavior, and respond to an evolving situation.

He tracked the bipedal cryptid's moves by the iron's reverb as claws tapped along the length. Setting up an echoing, discordant distraction from the left, then the right, switching randomly. Attempting to confuse the humans.

Hair lifted along Ridge's arms despite the sultry heat. This was no yearling ghoul, easy to fool and easy to dispatch. Only one that had survived repeated challenges during breeding season or battling for territory developed the skills to think through a fight, as opposed to charging in.

Ridge's stomach went into a free-fall. His teens were potentially facing a wily, seasoned killer.

A force like one of the island's ancient trees crashing during a storm sent palmetto leaves trembling, branches cracking, the impact thrumming up through the bronze and into the soles of his boots.

What truly looked like a caricature of a bipedal shark rose from the shredded greenery. Sandpapery gray skin and thick arms ended in wicked, hooked claws, silhouetted in the late sun's rays. The thing was nearly as wide as it was tall, puckered rows of scars and bite divots crisscrossing its thick body. Proof that Ridge's worst-case scenario guess was correct.

The ghoul roared, double rows of serrated teeth showing. It barreled straight at their position.

Gray and cream camo-clad bodies erupted from the pampas grasses around the statue. Cadets spilled out, knives flashing. Ridge's gut clenched, the kids looking even younger framed against the bulk of an adult male in its prime.

As half of the team met the creature, Ridge tapped his stopwatch on. Five minutes. They had five minutes to dispatch the murderous creature or again, the team failed the test. Their machete blades wove a beautiful pattern, moving in, slashing at the oblong face, then falling back out of close range.

Distracting it and allowing the third team member to dance in, swiping at its exposed flank. The cadets moved, retreated, flowed in and out in a perfectly choreographed pattern. Never in each other's path, never still.

Ridge's lips moved, silently running trough the commands he used on the training field like he could remind them.

Not too close. Grip firm but loose on the knife. Duck, duck, duck now.

The ghoul spun and claws *whoosed*, ghoul's bulging muscles putting enough force behind the strike to eviscerate a human. The kid lunged out of the way, but the rip of fabric tearing carried to Ridge. A claw tip catching sleeve.

At least lines of greenish-red blood now striped the cryptid's arms as well. Its ragged, stolen pants were in tatters, cuts from perfectly wielded knives opening along its thigh. It gave another roar, leaves rattling like a hurricane wind hit them.

Voice level, hiding both his pride and concern, Ridge warned them, "Time's nearly up. Finish this."

A ripple went through the fourth, positioned at the rear, the likeliest spot where a human might blunder into the fight, and the escape route the ghoul would try for if it bolted. His rifle stayed steady on the creature. Guns were a last resort in a populated area with the potential for civilian casualties. If the rest of the cadets failed to stop the ghoul, the sniper would, but yet again, the team would fail to graduate.

Ridge had done his damnedest to hammer in that survival was more important than passing. But they were trained to be relentless as hell, on top of their normal feeling of teenage invincibility and the adrenalin rush of fighting.

This, this was the point where their daring could get in the way of training. Where things could go so wrong. The dance of claws and blades in front of him picked up. Tempo increasing. So did Ridge's heart rate.

Cryptid blood spattered concrete and sand. But the cadet on the right hesitated. Ridge hadn't heard the tell-tale rip of clothing, but the red of human blood now coated the kid's hand. His knife wavered, and Ridge pulled and sighted down the barrel of his forty-five. Prepared to put a round through the ghoul's eye now, and worry about graduation grades after.

But as smooth as if they were linked, another dove in. Their knife slicing along the underside of the ghoul's upraised arm. The wounded cadet switched his knife to his off hand and rejoined the fray. Ridge still kept his weapon trained on the cryptid as his stopwatch counted down, second-guessing every exercise, every minute of class time they'd spent together. Whether he'd missed a key move, not made sure they understood a sequence before moving on to the next lesson.

The kid at the front stepped in, machete opening a gash on the ghoul's other arm as his teammate jumped in, blade slamming into the back of the ghoul's leg in the vulnerable joint. Then let go and rolled under the cryptid's vicious backhand, its frustrated roar rising again.

The front cadet flowed in, stepping into strike range. Right between the thing's arms. One misstep and the cryptid would snap her neck easy as breathing.

Ridge had taught them this, his signature move. Yet he still locked quivering muscles to keep from jumping in. She slammed her machete into the ghoul's chest. Her weight driving it in until no silver showed. She rolled clear, hitting the base of Ridge's perch, pushed off against it, and launched back at the ghoul. A second machete ripping free from her rig in a crackle of Velcro.

She came up under the thrashing creature, blade hitting the stomach and driving up, opening its abdomen.

The ghoul doubled over, slipping in blood as its bad leg gave. The team split up.

The one who had stabbed the ghoul grabbing the stair railing, vaulting up, and using the pipe as support. Then diving, both hands on the hilt, the blade pointed down. Razored metal rammed into the top of the ghoul's skull. Then continued, propelled by her momentum, tip punching through and coming out under its jaw.

The ghoul collapsed as she abandoned the blade, vaulting clear.

Tension flowed out of Ridge, like riding a barrel wave into the safety of the beach.

The pair responsible for the crippling blows exchanged a look, the rearmost one nodding.

"Stand down," ordered the front cadet, her voice sure and in charge.

The team all went from laser focused to relaxed.

"Good job." Ridge jumped from his perch, boots hitting the ground in a puff of sandy dirt and pure relief.

They answered in chorus. "Yes, sir!"

The foremost cadet, the team C.O., dug into a pocket on her tactical pants, pulled out a chunky phone and hit a number in a practiced motion, giving her I.D. number and the Company I.D., followed by a short, "Cleanup in progress."

Her team moved about, pulling weapons free from the carcass, another shaking out heavy black bags, putting bits of ghoul and sand contaminated with the greenish-red blood inside. Then the two on cleanup heaved the corpse and head into a second bag, the click of metal zipper teeth sealing away the evidence of cryptids among humanity. Today's mission had been hella public for a cryptid species that usually did its best to evade human detection.

"Reyes." First priority accomplished, the C.O. cornered her wounded teammate, who held out his gashed arm.

The team member designated as head medic bustled in, slicing away the torn sleeve and then turning to Ridge. "No tendons were involved, sir. Gel instead of stitches, right?"

"Right." He pulled his balaclava off, cooler air playing over his face in a welcome caress. "Remember to rinse it as clean as possible first, because who knows what carrion those claws had been digging in before attacking us."

Ridge's unmasking was the signal for the cadets to do the same. The C.O. cradled her teammate's arm as the medic squirted a packet of antiseptic rinse over it, grumbling. "Freaking nasty ghoul-gunk."

Four more urban camo-clad forms stepped from around the library's perimeter. All adults from Ridge's year group, the Regional team in charge of the mission-turned-cadet-exercise. They had stayed back, forming an escape-proof perimeter between the fight and any unexpected civilians with a sudden need to pick up library reading material. They would have also taken out the cryptid, if one of Ridge's nightmares had come true and the entire cadet team had been wiped out.

"Be glad it wasn't windigos." Ramirez—Vee, the Region Two C.O.—rolled her mask away, brown skin shiny with sweat, dark hair pulled back and into a knot. She gave Ridge a conspiratorial wink.

She was the smallest of the crowd but with the sort of presence that commanded attention. She had that thing, the one where she seemed ready to explode into action between heartbeats. "Those are *rank*."

Ridge laughed at the familiar complaint. "Commander Ramirez isn't wrong."

"Remember the one we accidentally exploded our last year as cadets?" Vee turned toward a much taller woman, otherwise similar enough to be her sister, and who was by Company standards.

Where Vee was contained kinetic energy, looking for a place to explode, her sister Liv gave the impression that she was always silently listing and evaluating threats. Unless you knew her and she'd let you into her circle, she was completely composed and by the rules. Even her hair was as perfect as when they'd left HQ, no flyaways or loose wisps, severe bun centered exactly at the nape of her neck.

Ridge took a saving-his-ass step back, way familiar with what came next. Also, way guilty.

"If by *we*, you mean Josh and Ridge playing with those sonic grenades, yes." Liv glared at their brother Josh.

The guy was the tallest of both groups, having several inches on Liv. Even with his basic, regulation fade, Josh was movie star pretty according to half of his and Ridge's class. He'd also joined Ridge in his fair share of pranks when they were all cadets.

"C'mon, Liv. You gotta let that go," Josh said and appealed to Ridge, no trace of his hidden side visible, the one who coolly looked through a scope and gauged the precise second to fire on his target. "Back me up here, man. No one told us that would happen."

"The grenades were prototypes." Ridge shrugged and grinned. "We were only furthering the research process. You can't hate on science."

Kimi, the last member of the Region Two team, snorted. A couple of the curls that had already escaped her bun haloed her heart-shaped face. A face Ridge might've had an epic crush on for a semester. Her fingers flew in the mix of ASL and Company signing she'd used since a ghoul took her voice their first year of live cryptid course work. "What you did was explode an already dead 'digo over us. It took days to get the smell out of our hair. *Days.*"

In an eerily similar fashion, all three of the female agents narrowed their eyes at him and Josh, clearly still holding a grudge.

"Like your brother said—you gotta let that go, Kim-ster." Ridge used the nickname he'd coined pre-crush. Then evaded Kimi's predictable retaliatory blow, dancing back out of range. Ducking behind Josh, both men still laughing. Reminding Ridge of how things had felt in their cadet days, before teams were made official and left for their new base. And he didn't.

With all evidence of the mission cleaned up and their teammate seen to, the cadets watched them like the older agents were a spectator sport.

"The moral of this story is, never wear your favorite body armor for a windigo call-out," Vee said to the entranced students.

"Yes, ma'am," they chorused again, awe evident. Vee's team was one of the best. Not just in the Southwest, but in North America, so Ridge got their fan-like reaction. Region Two was the team all the cadets wanted to be when they grew up. It was the team Ridge had once thought he'd be part of.

"It isn't official for a few more weeks but you guys aren't cadets anymore and you don't have to salute, and sir and ma'am us," Vee said.

Josh leaned in and fake-whispered, "You can't call her ma'am. Like, if *any* full team member, *anywhere*, slipped up like that with another Company agent… It's an insult. You know—it's like violating our code? Company doesn't thank Company." He quoted the line that represented how the Company was a family first and how they took care of each other.

The cadets darted glances at each other, probably weighing the unofficial motto they'd grown up with versus acknowledging rank.

It was a toss-up whether Ridge or Josh lost it first, their laughs booming out and mixing.

"Wow, your faces," Vee said.

"They're messing with you," Ridge translated for the cadets. Damn, they were graduates and able to efficiently take down a large predator, yet they still had so much to learn. So many things not in the rules or textbooks that he wished he could share.

They'd spend a couple of years shadowing an experienced team at least, learning real world details that even HQ's Academy couldn't teach, until they were assigned a sub-Region. Or a Region of their own if another team retired or was wiped out.

Ridge let go of that line of thought.

This was a good day, and the soon-to-be Company agents had nailed the mission.

"Clean up is complete and the area secure, sir." The cadet C.O. caught herself. "Uh—"

Ridge clapped her on the shoulder. "Don't sweat it. As for what's next, ask Region Two."

"Post-mission party," the four whooped and signed in unison. Their rituals as familiar to each other as breathing.

The cadets jogged after the departing team without another look at Ridge, all chattering as they piled into SUVs, while he brought up the rear.

The cadet team had been together since they were toddlers, like all teams. They were raised as siblings, despite biological differences. They knew each other inside and out. Now, they'd develop their own rituals and shorthand like all field agent teams.

He needed to focus on that, another team going out into the world to protect civilians, instead of the pang of envy at the cadets' closeness.

He'd done his duty. Trained the cadets for two years. Set them up for success, guided them through their first real mission, and could send them off with confidence in their skill and readiness. This was the third group he'd sent out so the kids' reaction wasn't a novelty for him.

He'd go back to Southwest HQ, and back to training teens to form the next Region stars. While he stayed on the outside, never having the intimate, tight knit sense of family. In an organization based on teamwork, he had no team.

He slid into the last truck and trailed behind the others to the post-mission graduation party. No way was he going to rain and angst all over their celebration, because these kids deserved better from him.

CHAPTER 2

M cKenna

I WATCHED a trio of excited tourists aiming cameras at a fin slicing through the Gulf waves, chattering about catching a video of a cute dolphin. Appearances were deceptive, though. Around here, fins usually meant bull sharks.

Metal bumped along weathered boards as Gabbi wrestled her chair around to catch a sliver of shade, automatically avoiding the larger patch cast by the table's umbrella. Not blocking my view when we were in an exposed, open area trumped escaping from the sun for both of us.

Gaze remaining on the strip of road separating the outdoor café from the beach, I raised two fingers over my head, trusting the waitress-slash-owner's daughter was on top of customer needs, since I was the only one at the moment. I spoke to my lunch date. "You're late, Miss Brat."

When I didn't get the standard snarky, 'I'm worth waiting

for' reply, I pulled my attention from watching for rivals, to the girl.

Since our last visit days before, she'd done rows of braids from temple to above her ear on one side, orange and red threads woven through her dark hair. The same color palette as my bleached and dyed hair ends, and the studs in my nostril. It was a cute style choice to the public, our crew's colors to locals.

Gabbi's marked her as under our—my—protection.

Today, her expression was that careful-neutral street kids learned early. Since she didn't have the giant hiker's backpack holding everything she owned, her silence wasn't stress over not having a relatively safe place to stay. Safe by her standards, not mine.

"¿Que onda?"

As food appeared in a gust of savory grilled grease and bright citrus, she cut a glance sideways instead of answering.

That she didn't jump on the carne asada before the waitress' hand completely cleared the plate told me how serious the kid's problem was.

The ever-present knot between my shoulders, where I carried my stress, jerked tighter but I picked up my drink and sipped. Pushing Gabbi didn't get any better results than pushing me had at that age. That streak of logic-defying stubbornness was half the reason we'd bonded.

"I come with a request," she blurted the second the server disappeared into the kitchen, still not meeting my eyes.

The lemonade turned to acid and I set my cup away. "I'm going to rewind and pretend the last thirty seconds never happened. Stop, think it through before you open your mouth again. Make sure it's worth what officially requesting Kane's aid will cost you."

Petitioning one of his enforcers was the same as asking him personally.

"Two of the kids are gone, McKenna."

Like Gabbi wasn't a kid herself.

Street kids being here one day, gone the next wasn't a new thing. Definitely not worth indebting herself to the Gulf Coast's reigning arms dealer.

Reading my mind, she glared at me, the effect undercut by her mindlessly picking at the already frayed hem of her cutoffs. "Neither of them were using, or dealing, or worked the corners, doing risky stuff, okay?"

I didn't miss that she referred to them in the past tense. "All right. Keep talking, but you're talking to *me*."

"One was wondering about calling an auntie. The other had a part time gig, and her boss said as soon as there was a full-time slot, it was hers."

"So theoretically, one went home, and the other's job could've come through and she got her own place," I said.

She gave a one-shouldered shrug, jaded expression at odds with her age. "I couldn't tell if her stuff was gone because she took it, or whether it got divided up once everybody decided she wasn't coming back."

Gabbi ran a tight ship with her bunch of found teens. There was only so much she could do, even when the penalty for breaking her rules was getting kicked out of the building she'd claimed, with its pirated electricity and my second hand protection.

"I'm sorry about your friends. You know that, but—"

"Liam didn't come home. We're—he wouldn't." Moisture shimmered in her eyes. Tears she'd never let fall in public.

Saying Liam and Gabbi had a thing was an understatement along the lines of saying Texas was warm in July. They'd been inseparable since the evening she had kicked a guy in the balls for threatening to bust Liam's guitar if the kid didn't hand over the money he'd made busking. After, she'd turned around and asked Liam to play her favorite song.

Liam had. Then he'd written a song for her, and that was that. They'd paired up almost three years ago, the same time I'd hit Kane's radar. I shoved my plate and drink aside and pulled out my phone. "When and where did you last see him?"

"Yesterday at the loft. He was tuning up for his gig at the bar. I had things to do but I was going to meet him after for pancakes and this sorta-party he'd texted about. Except he never showed up at our spot and he didn't come home."

I tapped in notes. "Did he make his set?"

If he hadn't made the performance, shit was dire. He and Gabbi couldn't pass up the under the table cash from playing, and he flat out wouldn't miss the opportunity to play at the dive bar frequented by talent agents and recording labels.

"Yes and he was awesome. The manager said Liam was the best—"

"Walk me through the rest. Did he hang out there after his set? Leave with anyone?"

The real teen hidden under the too-grown up shell peeked out, Gabbi rolling her eyes hard enough mine ached in sympathy. "No scouts were there and it was time to meet me, so he took the cash and left. Half-price pancakes wait for no one." She leveled a venomous glare. "He did not leave with anybody else. We're exclusive and we'd talk if we had a fight."

The kid was officially better adjusted than I ever hoped to be. "Send me a couple of recent pictures—clear shots that show his face."

She had the pre-paid phone I'd given her out and mine pinged with her texts almost before I finished my request.

"I'll have a couple of my guys do a sweep while I check around, and call hospitals. Do I need to tell you not to take chances with tourists?"

She snorted as answer.

With the influx of seasonal tourists came others harboring plans having nothing to do with dropping cash on rides at Moody Gardens, and shopping the historic district. Gabbi knew the risks but I couldn't help reminding her.

"When can I work for you?" Back on more familiar footing, she asked the same question as always.

I gave her the same answer. "Never. You can do better, and in a job that comes with dental and a travel allowance instead of jail time."

That was usually the sulky end to our discussion.

This time, Gabbi sat straight, gaze pinning me. "You've done good for yourself. You have a place, and a nice car, and friends, and you have power. People do what you say, and no one messes with you."

"Gabs—"

"If I worked for you, I could keep Liam and the house safe." Her gaze went to my middle and the gun concealed there.

"Eat." I rose, pushing her plate under her nose with one finger, while using my toe to nudge the backpack of what she called *monthly goods*, plus a few bucks, underneath her chair. "Call me if you hear anything I need to know."

I didn't have the words to explain or tell her how wrong she was. I had a little clout, earned with blood and ruthlessness.

I didn't have friends.

I definitely didn't have what she did with Liam and her house full of strays.

And I wasn't giving up on finding a means to convince her and her crew that they had brains, they had value, and they could rise above the crap that had been dumped on them. They just needed the opportunity.

"Hey, what do the missing two look like?" I asked

Displaying impressive multi-tasking skills, she shoved an avocado wedge in her mouth, flicking her phone on and scrolling through photos. She spun it around for me, as she drowned her tortilla in salsa verde.

I tapped the screen and the photo enlarged. A bunch of kids including Liam stood against the backdrop of the pier.

"There, on the end," she said.

I sent myself the photo, studying the missing girls. Both conventionally pretty, one with shoulder length braids and big anime cartoon-character eyes, the other with that perfect skin some teens managed, and inky ringlets. Thanks to Gabbi, they had avoided the worn look so many runaways had. They were almost as fresh-faced as Liam.

Maybe the girls had found their footing and moved on to better circumstances. There were other possibilities, though, especially for sweet-faced teens.

"Keep the phone close, stay together, and stay away from anyone you don't know. Pass the word." I tossed cash on the table and went looking for confirmation on an ugly suspicion about a new predator joining Kane's ranks.

* * *

I SMILED at the gym's reception person, aka one of the team's support staff, busy stocking clean towels. She waved and I kept going, through the door marked Employees Only. Continuing down the hall to the end, I keyed in my code on the access pad.

Instead of lockers, storeroom, or break area, the door opened on a windowless yet painfully bright room holding a long conference table. White boards filled with cryptic notes, photos, and arrows took up the wall space. A dozen of the region's LEOs—law enforcement organizations—from nearly as many agencies took up all the breathing room.

My arrival made it a baker's dozen, leaving me the odd number. Nothing new there.

For a joint task force the group was looking pretty damn divided. The local Violent Crimes unit was on one side, and Homeland on the other with FBI. ATF, my boss, stood at the head of the table.

He peered over the top of his glasses. For a guy who preferred Gucci to Kevlar, Freidricks exuded the kind of authority that had even the Homelanders quieting down. "Agent Cabello, finally check your watch?"

"Do people still wear those?" There was more than one reason Gabbi and I clicked.

Freidricks' nearly invisible white-blond brows inched up a centimeter. Enough of a chastisement that I automatically shut up and pushed through the local crew and the thick air of disapproval to join my wiry boss.

I didn't miss how they eyed my hair and piercings. Or how the crowd shifted, leaving the other officers suddenly unified and me alone except for Freidricks. Although he was ATF, he didn't count as *with me* in the same way.

He cleared his throat and the meeting began, Homeland jumping in with their report first.

Once upon a time, I'd found that air of arrogance and importance appealing. I listened to their rundown, watching the agent in the center of the group. I'd found Ryan equally appealing.

That clean-cut All American thing he was rocking, hair in *I rolled out of bed this way* waves, had been—exciting. And there was a chance he had felt like an achievement. I had the college degree, the kind of job people respected, and now, the guy that matched that aspiration.

I'd gone from unwanted foster kid people couldn't wait to get rid of, to someone who had a place and who belonged to something bigger.

That optimism hadn't lasted any longer than our relationship. When the shine wore off my job, revealing the tarnish, he'd cut and run before he was dulled by association.

Now, he faced forward, attention on his colleagues. His hands gave him away though, pinky flicking against his thumb non-stop, the tic that put in an appearance whenever he was nervous.

I caught his quick twitch when I shifted my weight, the squeak of three-hundred-dollar kicks against the generic flooring loud. The shoes, the mix of high-waisted athleisure pants, and tight designer jacket, were another marker of my alternate life. A slash of unwanted color against their khakis, polos, and button-downs.

It wasn't all Ryan's fault. No one had ever mistaken me for sweetness and light, especially in a fight. He also hadn't had any more seniority than I did, and maybe I wouldn't have risked my chances at advancement either if the situation was reversed. Rumors didn't need to be true to be devastating and have tangible consequences.

As the local Violent Crimes guy started in, I switched to paying attention.

"I'm closer to locating the organization's supply schedule code." The other undercover agent leveled his laser pointer at the board holding information, such as it was, on past shipments, locations, and buyers. Unfortunately, there were still gaping blank spots.

"Good work." Freidricks tipped his head at me. "What do you have for us, Cabello?"

The vibe of the room took a frostier turn.

The speaker and I were both undercover task force agents. That was where the similarity ended. He worked a laptop in one of Kane's numerous shell companies, trying to steal and decrypt information. His cover was a white-collar worker unaware who his employer really was, or what side-deals helped pay his wages. He got to keep his hands clean.

"Renee gave me another couple of streets to add to my territory roster." As I spoke, a poorly covered ripple of disgust went through the crowd. I'd have liked to believe it was over my bringing up the arms dealer in general, but in reality, it was my using Kane's first name and doing it so casually. My job required face-to-faces with the guy, and no pretty illusions of who I worked for.

I kept it professional. "He's had a series of meetings with his generals over the course of the last week, and Sims has attended every one. Sims has me working the streets, cracking down hard on anyone out of line and any talk, the same as the other generals are doing with their lieutenants. It's safe to assume Kane's ramping up for a new delivery."

"I can assume shit until the cows come home," one of the Violent Crimes set grumbled. "That doesn't make it accurate, actionable information though."

I counted to ten, not rising to the bait. I went over the same speech as always, countering the same criticisms and accusations that had been thrown my way numerous times by the people who were supposed to be my peers and backup. "Only his inner circle is privy to details. And that is a small, exclusive group from his college frat days."

"We've heard that before."

I talked over the interruption, not bothering to check on who said it. "I'm getting closer, though. Sims increasing my territory means Kane trusts me more. The next step is his circle."

"Yeah, and what's gotten you that extra shot of trust?" My more respectable counterpart asked.

There it was, the giant pink weapons-dealing enforcer-elephant in the room.

I leaned over the table, hands flat on the laminate surface

to keep them from bunching into fists. "You can't have it both ways, Jake."

"Cabello."

I straightened at Freidricks' reprimand. "Sir."

"This is a *team* effort. Stay on track, and continue."

"Yes, sir." Some of the *team* was simply more distasteful than others, though. "If a shipment is imminent, he'll tighten security on the streets and clubs. More sweeps equal more opportunities for me."

"Very well. Keep me informed in as close to real time as possible."

The crackle of disposable coffee cups and the swish of fabric marked the team calling the meeting done.

"One more thing, sir," I said and got a *go ahead* nod from my boss. "The chatter on the street is that people are going missing at a higher rate than usual. From the info I've pieced together they're young, attractive, and alone. I would like to consider the possibility that Renee or one of his generals has branched into human trafficking."

"By people, I'll take it you mean the homeless."

"Exactly. The kids—"

"Druggie runaways." The head of the FBI's lip curled under his mustache.

"*Kids*, yes. These are underage children. The rate is unusual, especially in such a short period."

"We are here for major arms trafficking routes and supply chains that lead to potential terror threats. Nothing else."

"If my suspicion pans out, it could be another avenue to pursue in identifying—"

"Or, it could be a Trojan Horse, a dead end to waste our time on and distract us from our primary objective so that we miss this deal," Jake, mister white collar, butted in. His tone left zero doubt he thought the latter, that I was the one pushing attention away from the incoming chance to I.D.

Kane's supplier, the bigger fish, the killer whale in our dangerous game.

Heat scorched my chest and cheeks. I looked to Ryan. We had discussed the possibility in passing before. Trafficking and drugs, along with weapons often went hand in hand, one paying for the other. If he backed me up—

He averted his eyes, stuffing his tie into his gym bag.

The silence went on a beat. Then Freidricks said, "Meeting over. Go find me hard information on this deal."

The looks that grated over my skin as the other agents left said it all.

I'd heard the whispers before. Could you *really* trust an agent who had been under as long as I head? Could you really trust one who calls a bad guy by name, who does awful things at his orders, who has blood on her hands from following them so well she had gone from an unknown street soldier to an enforcer in three short years?

That old saw about not being able to serve two masters, so which side is Cabello really on, hung unsaid.

As the hurt put my chest in a vice that felt like it should physically break ribs, I wondered how long I had until the officers who were supposed to be my team, my people, in a way those not in law enforcement could ever be, decided the answer was no.

That I was more criminal then agent.

I waited until the room cleared then left to follow my instincts. Since no one else would believe in me, I had to take my chances believing in myself.

CHAPTER 3

idge

RIDGE RESTED his butt and elbows on a huge length of driftwood that'd once been a tree, a remnant of the last hurricane lashing the Gulf Coast, watching the cadets celebrate as only Company could.

The four were engaged in a more than slightly inebriated game of volleyball. They'd drawn a ghoul's oblong face on the ball, with a red bull's-eye inked around it.

Mesquite-scented smoke drifted his way from the illegal barbecue pit he and Josh had tossed together, covering the salty tang of the ocean breeze. The day's heat was finally giving way to cooler air, sun drifting toward the horizon and putting on a display of pinks and purples. The fire pit gave a pop and crackle, and he shifted away from the sparks, taking a drink of already warm beer.

The cadet lieutenant with the ghoul wound spiked the

ball hard, and Ridge put fingers between his lips and whis-
tled his appreciation.

"You did a great job with them." From her spot on the end
of the log, Liv, hair still in its tight bun, leaned around Josh's
lanky form to address Ridge. "The team was solid today, and
the cadet C.O. and lieutenant were textbook perfect setting
up that attack plan and executing it." She held out her bottle
as did the rest of the team, and he tapped his in a chime of
glass on glass.

"They are—were—hella good students. That makes my
job easy."

"Nah, you've got the touch," Josh said. "You always have.
You're patient and can goof with them, and still keep them
focused."

Ridge left it at a shrug. The kids busted ass and earned
their success.

As a victory whoop came from the direction of the game,
one of them detached from the group. The boldest, the
reason she made C.O., took an open spot on a bench on the
other side of the fire pit.

"Nice work today," Liv said as greeting.

"It was standard ghoul one-o-one," the budding C.O. said,
but pride laced her tone.

Vee addressed her like she would any fellow C.O. "A
ghoul in broad daylight, off a busy street, is not standard
ghoul behavior."

"Man, don't get her started." Josh rolled his eyes. "It'll be
nonstop cryptid conspiracy theories all night."

Vee elbowed him. "It's not conspiracy if I'm right, and
cryptids *are* acting freaky."

"Anyway," Kimi signed, slower for the cadet's benefit.
"You guys were tight."

The new C.O. relaxed and addressed the Region Two

team. "Hey, is that legend about you guys taking down a vampire nest on your graduation exercise true?

"It was only two vampires," was all Vee said, like that wasn't impressive as hell all on its own.

"It was supposed to be a basic windigo horde op, right? Eliminate them before they got from the desert to populated areas, and before their stink drew notice. But then we stumbled over these vampires as we were mopping up, and *that's* when things got crazy," Josh tagged in.

In what seemed like seconds, the rest of the volleyball team had joined the circle around the pit, listening to the teams' stories.

Hanging on every word.

The cadet lieutenant accepted a beer from Kimi. "I hope we get assigned to your Region. We studied your technique on patrolling windigo migrations, and our medic has a sixth sense for when a horde will hit." He tipped his bottle at a stocky blond kid beside him. "He's our go to. It's time to get out of school and on to the important stuff."

Ridge stood, offering his spot to the blushing cadet medic.

Josh frowned, the expression alien on the habitually chill agent, and leaned backwards from the group. "Food's almost ready, and I say we turned that rack of ribs into heaven on a plate."

"I'll be back soon. Just need to take a walk to get the kinks out," Ridge said. "Save me a plate, yo? You owe me one for that high quality fiction I spun about the sonic grenade."

His grin must not have been convincing, a shadow of pity passing over Josh's face. His friend slapped on a fake smile, holding out knuckles to tap. "Solidarity. Your ribs are safe with me."

"I know what a big ask that is." Ridge saluted, and picked a random direction, not acknowledging the sting of always being seen as second-tier, less-than. The real hurt though was not having that easy intimacy of teammates.

The family ties, and finishing each other's sentences, that was what a team was all about. People knowing you inside and out and having your back no matter what, from birth to death.

The animated chatter and savory smokiness of grilling beef faded behind him. The crunch of sand under his soles and the muted rush of waves kept him company.

Shit, he got why cadets didn't think the Academy was exciting. If he checked the records moldering away in the archives, he was sure the attitude went back as far as humanity organizing into what would officially become the Company, same in every branch from the South Pacific to Siberia. Civilian school students probably felt the same, although he doubted their curriculum included cryptid biology, tracking, and sniper training. Or that their labs involved canned hunts with ghouls and windigos brought in and released on training grounds.

He hadn't thought their old instructors were boring. They were primarily teams that made it to retirement. The occasional survivor of a horrific team disaster. But he—all of his year group including Josh, Vee, and their siblings—had also been awed by instructors' experiences as Regional teams.

He'd never had those experiences. Training exercises, sure. The graduation jobs, and occasional missions when teams joined together for something big, and when extra hands were needed, were it. A few missions busting gladiator-style cryptid fighting rings, where all sorts of predators were featured, including those native to other regions, windigo hordes, the rare vampire nest.

Those sucked since vampires weren't true cryptids but humans mutated by a virus. The virus was a natural occurrence though, and someone, somewhere back in the day, had decided, *hey, close enough.*

He'd done his share, and done it well.

But he'd never had real team siblings. Those started coalescing when cadets were children, when groups gravitated together, when kids' specialties were identified and encouraged. Each team needed at a minimum a C.O., a lieutenant, a tech person, and medic. He'd been friends with everyone, snipers were always in demand, and that was his *thing.*

He'd been floated from emerging group to emerging group. But that organic slotting into a family never happened. He became an instructor straight out of Academy.

The anomaly who'd never been a team member. So even now, he didn't quite belong among the other trainers. He never doubted the friendships or that the Company valued him the same as other agents, but teams were raised as siblings, meant to fill all emotional needs, and here he was, an only child.

He huffed a silent laugh.

Man, he was *all over* the drama today. Major drama llama was what Liv, Vee, and Kimi always called it back in the day, when they all watched civi shows and movies.

He shoved his hands in his pockets, the action pulling his concealed holster snug, head tilted back. The moon was waning, but no clouds dimmed its glow. He'd gone further than he intended, and away from the surfside restaurants and hangouts. Instead of salt, it felt like the breeze here carried a tang of diesel and oil, leaving an almost greasy film on his skin.

The moonlight reflected off windows, most dark at this hour, utilitarian docks, and the metal of shipping containers and industrial equipment. Out of the rows of buildings only one had any signs of activity, unforgiving halogen light from an arched window. The glow highlighted a black and white logo with *RK Imports* in simple lettering underneath. A Jeep, truck, and motorcycle were parked off to the side.

The door opened, a guy walking out with his back to Ridge.

A second later the door opened and shushed closed again. Voices rose in the back-and-forth of conversation, one feminine. He turned to rejoin his cadets' celebration, leaving these late workers to whatever their jobs demanded.

Under the conversation, a metallic *skree* echoed.

A twin to the one he'd heard during the training mission. The sound of claws drawn along concrete.

Ridge concentrated, blocking out far off traffic sounds, the muted lap of water, the low conversation. The noise repeated, coming from out past the cars and around the corner. The same spot as where the workers had gone.

He sprinted, shoes soundless as sand gave way to asphalt. His gun was in his hand, natural as breathing. He hit the corner, his back to the wall as a scream shredded the night.

The ghoul crouched atop a dumpster. A body hung impaled on his claws. The man who'd exited the business first, his heels drumming against the dumpster, frantic *bongs* replacing conversation.

The other employee, the woman, had a gun out, holding it like she'd logged plenty of time on the firing range. She was moving in a careful shuffle. Keeping her attention on the cryptid. Trying for clearance to take a shot.

The creature lifted the body, using it as a shield. The man screamed again, ending in a raspy, wet cough.

Fuck.

The dumpster was backed against another building. Wedged between the L-shape created by the building and a solid security fence. Too tall for the cryptid to scale carrying prey. Its only way out was through the woman.

Unless Ridge could change its mind.

This ghoul was half the size of the one from the library. But its tough hide took a hell of a lot more than the small HK, the regular off-duty weapon Ridge carried, or even the Glock the woman held. If she fired, it would only anger the ghoul, which would tear through her escaping.

Keeping his tone calm and authoritative as he would with first-year cadets, Ridge said, "Don't move, and don't shoot."

The woman swore in Spanish. Then switched to English. "Get out of here. Back up, then call nine-one-one. Ask for an ambulance, and SWAT." Even facing something that probably looked like a nightmare come to life, she didn't flinch, voice as professional as his.

A spurt of appreciation went through Ridge. "Ma'am, plain rounds won't kill the target."

The ghoul snarled, backing against the wall, hefting the wounded man, whose head lolled, claws peeking through his chest. Ridge could tell the guy was no longer moving, even from a yard out.

Anger settled in Ridge's gut. The male civilian was past saving. He wasn't letting the woman come to the same end. "Listen, your friend is dead, okay?"

"I fucking know that." Her tone held an echo of the anger in his.

Ridge eased a step forward.

The ghoul tensed. Earless oblong head moving back and forth. Evaluating which way to dive for freedom—through the woman or through Ridge.

It wasn't protocol, but if he could get close enough for a kill shot—

"Ma'am, you need to step aside. Slowly, and behind me."

"I'm not letting that—that—whatever it is get loose to murder every third-shift security guard or worker between it and freedom."

Respect for the civilian willing to go head-to-head with a cryptid to protect people edged out Ridge's anger. Respect at her fierceness, too. A second and he had his holster's other occupant out, its razor-sharp edge gleaming, and in his free hand.

"Same page, ma'am." The next part could go hella wrong. "Our rounds are only going to annoy it at this distance. I need a distraction, something to let me get close."

"Fine. I'm ready."

The creature crouched. Its muscles bulged, threatening to rip the too-small pants it likely stole from its last victim as primitive camouflage. The trick they used to scavenge among humans when corpses, their natural food source, were scarce.

"Now," Ridge ordered, and launched.

The rapid bark of shots followed him. The body the ghoul held jumped, not from life but from impact of the brilliant woman's shots.

She'd have pissed the cryptid off if she'd aimed at it, but hitting the body—the ghoul froze for a heartbeat, confused.

Ridge grabbed the edge of the dumpster and jumped. The creature spun, clumsy and hampered by the body. Ridge aimed for the ghoul's eye. His blade hit the hard ridge over it instead, skin splitting, but the knife bouncing.

The attack served to take the animal's attention off Ridge's civilian.

The ghoul reared, slinging the dead body off in the same motion.

Ridge ducked, body sailing past him. Then came up inside the creature's reach, same maneuver he taught the cadets. Slamming his knife in the exposed eye. Bringing the HK against the other at the same time.

Gray arms closed around him. Crushing. His vision going

spotty, lungs screaming. He squeezed, bullet slamming into its remaining eye. The creature roared, blocking out the sound of gunfire, the combination leaving Ridge's head ringing.

Off balance, he tilted. Ground rushed to meet him as the ghoul attempted to jump, its brain already fritzing, and falling instead. Taking Ridge with it.

The impact rattled through him, his skull bouncing off the ghoul, the diamond grit skin scouring his bare arms and legs. He got a knee under him and heaved, knocking the twitching body off, until he could push free. A clawed arm lifted, half speed. Aiming for his face. He grabbed the knife hilt and rammed it in until it hit bone.

The ghoul went limp.

Motion flickered in the corner of his hazy vision and he shoved away, getting his feet under him again. Reaching and bringing the gore-coated knife with him, ready for a new threat.

His civilian was standing over him, gun steady on the ghoul. Her other hand was held out to him, her lips moving.

He shook his head, pointing at his ears, hearing temporarily gone thanks to the shots and ghoul vocalizing in his ear. He dropped the knife, concentrating on lip reading—really nice lips, too—full and shiny but natural colored. He made out "Okay?"

"I'm fine," he said—bellowed, probably. He palmed his phone, flicking the sturdy case open, tapping in nine-one-one to Vee, but watching the woman. Several inches shorter than him, with curved brows darker than her hair, arching over big brown eyes. She'd lined them, making them look even bigger and more expressive. And not one drop of panic or fear in them.

Despite the gun and her obvious expertise with it, her

short, snug jacket basically served as a frame for her breasts. Some intricate, strappy thing under it more a bra than a shirt, and those athletic pants that weren't really meant for a gym hugged her waist and hips.

The contrast between the sexy, impractical clothes and her unflappable, nerves-of-pure-titanium demeanor intrigued the hell out of him for some reason.

Basically drooling over a civilian vic definitely wasn't Company conduct though. He quickly redirected his attention, and libido.

The woman's lips were still moving, and he squinted, glad of the time he'd put in learning to read Kimi's. He made out "…damn idiot. What were you thinking?" and a laugh rattled his chest. Because yeah, she was fierce as hell. Then he winced, bruised ribs complaining at his amusement.

"I called for—" he caught himself "—for the authorities, okay? They'll be here in a few. You're safe now."

She glared, but crouched beside him, her hand hovering over his face, then moving down. The motion graceful, delicate fingers ending in short but glittery nails, she pointed at his chest.

He glanced down. His shirt was covered in goo and blood. She must've caught his earlier wince. No way did he want to worry her. "No biggie," he said-bellowed again. "See?"

She kept her gun out but held it pointed down, other hand grabbing the hem of his shirt, a question in her eyes. Concern visible in their melty-brown depths.

"Go for it." He lifted his shirt. Then warm, competent hands slide over his ribs and chest. It felt like a current arced between them when they touched. Not painful though. Electrifying in the same way as catching and riding the perfect barrel wave.

She hesitated, lips parted, like maybe she'd felt—whatever this was. Then ducked her face away, continuing her gentle, self-appointed task. She hit an already forming bruise but he held still. Busy watching her, and the firm line of her jaw. Colorful hair swung against his cheek as she examined him, and he caught a whiff of spice and citrus, then lost it again under the acrid stink of dead ghoul.

Something glinted against the smooth brown skin of her face. Jewels. Two tiny, faceted studs in her left nostril, one red, the other orange. Small, twisted gold hoops hung from her ears.

No one in the Company had piercings, even ears, and hers fascinated him almost as much as her courage had. Without checking in with his brain first, his hand was somehow an inch from her cheek.

She must've seen the same question in his eyes as when she'd silently asked permission to touch him, because she tilted her head that last fraction. Then his thumb was skimming along her cheek. He glided the pads of his fingers over the arc of whatever barely-there shimmer she'd dusted along her cheekbones, giving her a glow like the moon hid just under her skin. He winced when his rough callus caught against her smooth perfection.

She didn't pull away, her open hand resting in the middle of his chest.

Movement where there should only be darkness registered, and Ridge rolled to his feet, shoving her safely behind him with one hand, grabbing the knife with the other.

A man slowed, gun in hand and aimed at them. His civilian stepped around Ridge with her hand out. His hearing was coming back, enough that he caught "Don't" and "cops coming."

Gun-guy swore and got animated, arms waving like he'd

forgotten he held a weapon, and panic on his narrow face. She turned, hesitating a second, concerned gaze on Ridge like she wasn't through checking him over.

The other guy got shriller. She swore and grabbed the guy's arm, hauling him after her, shoving him in the Jeep.

Damn it.

Ridge sprinted for the vehicles, because these were witnesses. She might need counseling despite her seeming strength and composure. Plus they required debriefing by HQ, but the car turned over, headlights flashing on.

She looked back at him, over her shoulder and the expanse of bloody parking lot. Their gazes locked for a heartbeat.

As her passenger's volume rose, and the car reversed, speeding off, he settled for memorizing the tag number, and standing guard over the ghoul that couldn't fall into civilian hands.

The Company's first mandate was protecting civilians, at all costs. Part of that was preventing cryptids like the ghoul, ripe for exploitation, from coming to public knowledge. The Company defended against cryptid abilities ever being leveraged to create chaos and terror, destabilizing the human world.

He still strained, craning his neck as far as he could, watching until the woman was out of sight.

* * *

WITH HQ's FREEZING A/C turning his sweat and the ghoul gunk dried out and itchy, Ridge stared at the laptop screen. Like the words would somehow rearrange themselves. The description beneath the photo of his civilian—McKenna Cabello—didn't change.

Nor did the description of her suspected crimes. A stint

in human juvenile detention, and a string of petty crimes after. The list changed in type and severity three years ago, to more serious suspicions of racketeering, assault, and weapons smuggling.

There it was, her photo with deep brown eyes and shiny perfect lips, hair like a bonfire come alive, right beside that of Renee Kane, Ivy League graduate and suspected arms dealer. Both under scrutiny by a whole alphabet soup of human law agencies.

She was an up and coming soldier for the state's most dangerous criminal. *She* was a criminal.

"Man, guess that explains why she was armed and didn't immediately melt down," Josh said from the chair he'd appropriated out of one of the myriad of HQ's other office suites.

Josh's voice was tinny, but most of Ridge's volume aftereffects had vanished. He cracked his jaw, trying to pop his ears.

"That was on-point work, taking out a ghoul one-on-one," Liv said, giving him one of her real smiles, the one that hinted at the daredevil under her professional mask.

"I had some help."

They'd left the ghoul and attack site to the Cleaners, the HQ branch who sanitized cryptid crime scenes, the party cut short by Ridge's call. Now that everyone was back at HQ, the festivities had rekindled out on the hunt field, fire pit exchanged for a grill, the beach for manicured grass and trees.

From his standing desk, Miguel glanced back at them. "You're positive the second civilian didn't see the ghoul?"

"Yeah positive. We—I—was between him and the carcass, and the dumpster shielded the rest."

His year mate and best friend grunted. "We'll keep eyes

out for any chatter, but bringing those two in is too complicated an undertaking versus potential reward."

Meaning, the Company wouldn't raid whatever safehouses the dealers owned, not that they'd have done it directly, but via agents within other government or law groups. There weren't many means open to this witness as far as spewing the truth about what she'd seen, not without opening up a can of worms and drawing attention she or her boss wouldn't want. The site was also now pristine with no sign of the creature or a fight to corroborate her story if she did talk.

The civilian casualty would also be officially noted as anything but a cryptid cause of death. Probably gunshot from a mugging gone wrong.

McKenna wouldn't be pursued unless she caused a stir.

Ridge shouldn't care. But the idea of her being punished —it didn't sit well with him. He definitely hadn't single-handedly taken down that ghoul. McKenna had helped, his accidental partner emptying her weapon into the body to buy him time.

The idea that the brave, capable person he'd observed—because ninety-nine-percent of civilians, even LEOs, would've freaked when confronted by a creature that wasn't supposed to exist—was one of the bad guys also didn't sit well.

The person who tried saving her friends, and who had worried over Ridge. Taking time and care to check him out after seeing blood on him. What civilian did that after a horrific cryptid encounter?

Her touch still clung to his skin.

"That's another ghoul, the fourth in two weeks," Vee said, pulling him out of his ...whatever.

Josh groaned. Even Kimi and Liv rolled their eyes.

"Hello? Secretive scavengers suddenly hard-core hunting,

and not the usual tent cities but in *daylight* and in heavily populated centers. The one today choosing to engage with a group of armed humans instead of bolting." Vee paced a loop around Miguel's modest office.

A single ghoul and single death didn't rate the main command center and multiple researchers' attention. Just Miguel in Surveillance.

"It doesn't follow typical ghoul behavioral patterns." Miguel spoke while pulling up activity reports, probably the ones detailing species activity. Multiple tabs popped up, like playing cards fanned across a table.

"See?" Vee pointed at Ridge's brother, then her team.

"I can keep an eye on it," popped out, Ridge's mouth not checking with his brain.

They all stared at Ridge. Waiting for the punch line.

This time he wasn't goofing. "It'll be a couple of weeks until I get my next class. I can patrol until then. Might as well use me." There. That was an excellent reason.

Definitely having nothing to do with McKenna Cabello and unanswered questions.

Miguel deferred, looking to Vee. "Do I put in a note?"

Josh stretched and rose. "Don't sweat it. This is a one-off thing. Plus, we've got it if not. Take the downtime while you can, my brother. You've got another couple years of twenty-four-seven cadet duty waiting for you."

"Truth." Liv motioned for them all to follow her. "The team will handle it if anything pops up—it's our job. There better be some cake left," she said in a lightning change of topic.

"Shower first," Kimi signed, eyeing him and his filthy tee and shorts. "We'll save you a piece. Probably."

Absently nibbling at a cuticle, Vee hung back, brow furrowed and staring at the screen. Somehow he doubted the human on the screen was her focus though. She finally sighed and turned. Shoulder-bumping him she said, "Seriously, take the downtime, Ridge. And hurry, because 'probably save' really means a cake-less night."

Ridge got it.

They were the agents.

He was a temp, and no longer needed.

CHAPTER 4

$\mathcal{M}$cKenna

I MIGHT BE SEATED in front of my boss, and he might've sounded forbidding as hell on the call demanding my presence ASAP. That didn't mean I had to revert back to acting like a kid busted by the principal. Taking a cleansing breath, I forced muscles to relax, uncrossing my arms and resting my hands in my lap.

I tried approaching the conflict from a different angle. "Sir, I know what I saw."

Still standing, Freidricks took his glasses off, and centered them in the middle of his immaculate desk. Then pinched between his brows.

When he finally looked at me, I got a view at the bags under his eyes. "Cabello, what the hell am I supposed to do with a report claiming an 'approximately six foot gray skinned creature' attacked one of the primary shell businesses owned by the subject of a years-long, multi-departmental sting, leaving one of his generals missing and—"

"He isn't missing. Sims was dead, and barely in one piece."

"*Missing*, because there was no body nor evidence of an altercation. What we do have, is confirmation from you that Kane thinks last night was an attack on him, and that he may be postponing. Our chatter says he is considering potentially even moving it to an offshore location. We have minimal intel where, not to mention the issue of jurisdiction, much less mobilizing assets should we gain a green light. Am I wrong on any part of this summary?"

I slumped in the chair. He wasn't wrong.

I'd been at the docks trying to get some kind of insight on the organization's foray into human trafficking, a yes or no, from Sims, the general I reported to. I'd been hard pressed to stomach the things I'd said, approaching the question as a pitch to diversify the business.

What I'd gotten was uncharacteristic evasion, and when I'd followed Sims outside, a freaking nightmare. That, and a dead member of Kane's blood brotherhood. The bond he'd shared with Kane was the reason I'd targeted and attached myself to Sims. He was my in into that exclusive circle.

All ruined by an implausible nightmare.

I'd been there.

I'd seen the creature eviscerate Sims. Then witnessed the big blond jump in and tag-team, taking the thing down with a skill and familiarity that set off all sorts of warning bells. And I still doubted what happened.

Freidricks cleared his throat, the short reminder holding a world of subtext.

"No, you aren't wrong. Kane is out for some serious blood over Sims." I leaned in, butt leaving the seat, like I could push conviction into Freidricks. "Except—"

"Tell me there was no creature. Tell me there's a logical,

palatable reason Kane's most trusted general is MIA, and a bottom feeder street soldier under you command swears there was an attack and police called, when no such call record exists. While you're at it, tell me you weren't there pursing this trafficking angle I plainly forbade you to touch." Frustration leaked out around his composed edges, and he stood, wiry but towering over me. "Let me help you, McKenna."

"I'll find out what last night's attack was. I'll get you—something."

Freidricks sat and slapped his laptop open. "I am writing it up as a masked, unknown assailant. That won't fly for long, though. Get the sale information. Give Kane something to work with, some real target that will keep him and this meet on track. And quickly, before there's nothing I can do for you."

He watched me, his expression altering. "You are good—there was a reason I recruited you straight from the academy. However, you've been under for years, and even older, experienced agents would feel that stress. After such intense immersion—the lines of who you owe loyalty to can blur." He picked up his glasses and jammed them on.

Seconds ticked by. When he didn't look up from his new report, I rose and let myself out to the angry click of computer keys.

I didn't need the implication spelled out.

The rest of the force thought I'd staged the disappearance. Best-case scenario, going rogue with my own unsanctioned plan to get closer to Kane.

Worst case, I'd done it to get into Kane's inner circle for my own personal benefit. Using it as the opportunity to foul the task force by warning Kane, because I was a dirty cop.

Hell, it's exactly what I would've thought, if I was on the outside looking in.

I left the quiet gym, sun blinding me for a moment and the heat wrapping around me like an unwanted blanket. I slammed the Jeep door hard enough the car rocked, then rested my forehead on the wheel.

Apparently overhearing Mister Hottie McSave the Day's comments as I checked that he hadn't been mortally injured fighting the creature, that little weasel Markie had babbled about a cop and police en route. The idiot was on the phone before we'd even cleared the docks. And before I could warn him to keep his mouth shut so I could spin the disaster. Preferably by using the slimy little suck-up, who'd been all over my hints at brutalizing and selling other human beings, as the scapegoat.

Now I had more problems than time. Kane and the crew fired up, just fucking looking for a reason to start a street war. The deal that could finally blow the case wide open either tabled or outside our reach. The task force leaning harder into the McKenna-is-a-dirty-cop angle. My boss and only ally edging toward the decision to bench me due to mental health concerns.

Worst of all, I had a horrific idea that the kids hadn't disappeared into a trafficking ring but rather down the throat of some impossible monster.

I slammed the car in gear and went to find some answers.

* * *

I PACED our parking lot for the third time. No body, of course. Also, no bloodstains, and no casings. The place wasn't simply clean, it was freaking spotless. Even the skid marks I knew I'd left peeling out of the lot had vanished. The dumpster was also brand new, without the dent in the left corner from Sims accidentally backing a forklift into it. There was most definitely no caved-in lid where the alleged figment of my imagination landed, or the gouges where its claws had dug in.

The site had been cleaned, and by someone with the expertise and tech to professionally process and wipe a crime scene.

My number one suspect was the guy who'd charged in like an avenging hero, not batting an eye at seeing a CGI special effect come to life, and who had calmly tossed together a plan in seconds. The same guy who'd gone hand-to-hand with the monster.

More telling, he'd won.

Instead of interrogating him like a professional, I'd…not swooned, because the word, the entire *concept,* was definitely not part of my vocabulary. Or reality. He was simply a bystander who I, as an officer of the law, had of course been concerned about. One who didn't hesitate to help people.

I didn't need to know what the monster-thing was to understand I'd been blocking its escape route. The guy had chosen to put himself directly in the monster's path instead. I couldn't remember anyone ever willingly taking a hit meant for me.

The way he'd stared at me after—he hadn't been angry or even annoyed that he'd been beat to crap on my account. Instead, he'd seemed fascinated.

A ghost of the full-body shiver I'd experienced when he cradled my check flowed through me.

Enough. Obsessing over a guy wasn't happening. I'd learned my lesson with Ryan, that people didn't and wouldn't look past my surface, and put the work in to get to know me. It was a repeat of my childhood and foster care.

Last night's violence, as it pertained to my job, was priority one.

I grabbed my drink and the street corn I'd stopped at a food truck for and stood in the sliver of shade cast by the awning. I let my brain do its thing, the fight replaying in slow motion in my head.

The guy had come in at an angle to me, to my right.

I chewed and moved to the spot I'd been at the night before, then turned, arm and corn held straight out. Visually following that line, I catalogued what lay along the route. Since last night's monster weirdness aside, I wasn't buying that the guy was some merman who'd surfaced from under the docks, that only left the beach to the west as his origin.

This section of sand and surf was relatively tourist-free because it wasn't highlighted on most of the maps. It was a popular hangout for locals, especially those who knew beach patrol rarely hit the area. Meaning they wouldn't get rousted for bonfires, grilling, and having open containers of alcohol.

The strip of beach eventually fed into the docks and our warehouse. I drifted in the direction Mister Mystery had come from. I'd hit up our databases on the slim chance he was a snoop for a rival organization but a quick search of the files hadn't brought up any matches.

Which left me out of options, other than magically getting lucky. I snorted at that idea, then sneezed, my swallow of soda fizz going the wrong way.

A shape loomed over me and I let go of the bottle, reaching for my weapon. Cursing myself for getting so in my head that I forgot what and where I was, and the always-present potential for violence.

I came up sighting on a blond head, now at my waist level. Blondie was on one knee with my soda bottle in his hand, saved from shattering on the ground.

The Good Samaritan with the uncanny reflexes looked up.

"Oh, you have got to be kidding me." I glared down at Mister Mystery.

Laugh lines crinkled at the corners of his blue eyes, fringed by thick, darker lashes.

"Hi." He smiled, a dimple popping into existence. He held the bottle out to me.

When I didn't move or lower my gun, his smile faded. The absurdity of holding a gun on a guy only armed with an orange soda registered, and I holstered my piece.

He stood, and I revised my mental statement to include armed with my soda, a dimple, and a ton of muscles. I hadn't been sure about what I'd seen under his shirt post-attack, aside from knowing he obviously worked out, more concerned about possible wounds.

In the morning sun, I confirmed he was working a six-pack. At least.

The athletic cut tee clung to an expanse of chest and defined abs, sleeves snug around ridiculously cut biceps. "No freaking wonder you could vault onto a dumpster."

Heat blistered my cheeks since that hadn't quite come out the way I intended.

That dimple made a reappearance. "You were all over it, too."

I stepped out of charm range. Like a foot of breathing room would turn me back into an adult with a functioning brain, banishing my hormonal teen reaction. "Excuse me?"

"Uh, I mean the cryptid. Last night. With the not panicking? Firing to distract it was some fast thinking." His smile dropped, turning him into the controlled, competent person who had led an attack on a monster. "I'm sorry about your friend. I didn't get a chance to say that or ask if you were all right."

"I wasn't the one going MMA on a—"

"Cryptid."

"On a cryptid." I tried out the word. "Nor was I nearly flattened when it fell on me."

"Nah, I'm sturdier than I look."

No shit.

Time to get this conversation back on track. I plucked the drink from him and strode to the dumpster, standing on tip-toes to flip the lid, and tossed my lunch inside.

I spun around, the guy right at my heels, crowding me. I caught myself for the second time today and uncrossed my arms. "Now, let's talk about the fact that there was zero mention in the media of a shooting or a body found, continue through how it seems as if the cartoon T.V. commercial cleaning guy went to town on our business space," I rapped my knuckles on the dumpster "and finish with *what the hell* a cryptid is, where it came from, and why it was here. Go." I pointed at him.

Forgetting both how close he was and how much there was of him, my finger poked downy shirt and the sculpted chest underneath.

With him square in front of me and the dumpster at my back, I had no room to retreat.

Like he understood, he took several steps sideways and rubbed at the back of his neck as if he was embarrassed. "Sorry. I always forget about civ—uh, regular personal space requirements."

Whatever he'd been about to say, it wasn't *regular*. And I wasn't letting him blush and dimple-cute his way out of answering me. "Cryptids, remember? Let's begin there. That thing was called a cryptid? Where is it from? Why was it here and attacking people?"

"This isn't an ideal spot for that discussion. How about your office?" He glanced at the RK building.

So he knew I technically worked there. Yeah, dimple-guy was more than he appeared. His plain tee and cargo shorts felt like as much of a costume as my red and orange color palette and street style.

He must have taken my silence as a problem since his eyes widened. "We can go somewhere else. Or stay out here. I get you don't want to be alone with some strange guy who kinda kills things."

Fear wasn't at all what I'd felt in his presence. I jangled my key ring at him and walked to the office, unlocking the door and holding it open.

He trotted in without another word. I closed the door and followed. Then hit and bounced off a broad back and entirely too chiseled ass where he'd stopped without warning just inside the threshold.

He turned in the same sort of smooth burst of strength as when he'd attacked the creature, catching my waist, like he was keeping me on my feet.

His hands were warm and strong. Same as his touch the evening before. That same out-of-nowhere excitement tingled across my skin. Callused palms brushed my stomach where the cropped bustier and bellyband holster ended. My nipples pebbled and I shivered.

He let go fast. "Ahh, hell. Sorry, ma'am."

"McKenna Cabello." Back on safer ground, I relaxed. He'd clearly already done his homework and I was listed publicly as manager at RK Imports. I wasn't telling him anything he didn't already know. "And?"

He blinked at me. Then that dangerously open smile was back. "Ridge Prescott."

Of course. He would have an All American, ritzy Anglo name to match the blond hair and blue eyes. He'd probably also been voted Most Popular and a soccer captain or star football quarterback. For all I knew, he still was, the lighter streaks in his dark blond hair the product of time spent under the sun, not in a salon chair.

His attention wandered, and so did he, ambling from the small chair and loveseat that served as our waiting area, around the pair of desks, then poking his head through the opening to the warehouse bay. Not that there was anything to see. This company did function as an import biz, although it also laundered Kane's money in doing so.

He was disarmingly affable, on top of being a walking fitness ad.

An ideal cover, if he was from a rival organization thinking to move in on Kane's customer base. His curiosity also made sense were that the case. My hand drifted back to my gun.

Then I caught myself. Tossing some sort of a killer pet at us in order to get invited into a business that anyone could stroll into between the hours of nine and five was even less plausible then the monster-pet actually existing.

"Cryptid?" I prompted him.

"Right. That."

"Spit it out. Was that some kind of Jurassic Park prehistoric DNA project gone wrong?" Because that was my best guest. If there were tiny creatures discovered in rainforests yearly, and things scientist thought were extinct washing up on shores, logic dictated this cryptid thing could be one more such find. Ideally, the last of its kind.

"No, nothing like that."

Shit. If the logical option was out, then that didn't leave much. "Was that a spirit? And do not lie. I had a foster parent who smudged the apartment and lit candles and saw balls of light on the mountainside and watched birds for omens. I thought she was a fanatic, but now—"

He stepped in front of me making the universal time-out sign. My guess about his playing some team sport was completely correct.

I glared. "Information, Prescott. Now."

For some reason that brought on a crooked grin. "Here's the deal. That wasn't reconstituted dinosaur DNA or a lab experiment or any kind of ghost. There's a whole Latin species name, but we—I—go with ghoul."

Again with the hesitation. He wasn't lying but he was editing information. I made a *keep talking* motion.

His grin grew. "Man, you are one cool customer."

More like I'd had multiple classes in psychology, interrogation techniques, and hostage negotiations. And I damn well knew what I'd seen. "Waiting."

"Cryptids are just animals. All natural. Some are larger and predatory, some only pests. Texas has ghouls and windigos, mostly. Windigos are sorta canids. Oh, and they stink."

He seemed to think he was done, satisfaction rolling off him like cologne.

"So to recap, you are saying there are animals out there, some lethal, that have seemingly evaded detection by, oh, I don't know, the general public, scientists, reporters, and random teenagers with cell phones."

He nodded, beaming like I was his favorite student.

"Yet these critters have names straight out of folktales and mythology," I continued. "That accurate?"

"Pretty much, yeah. Listen, I know it sounds wild but—"

I held up a finger, taking a play from his book. "Let's skip the part where you try to convince me of what I saw. There's nothing wrong with my vision, reasoning skills, or brain." Despite my boss entertaining the theory I was suffering from PTSD or psychosis. "That ghoul was most definitely real, Sims is most definitely dead, it bled and we were able to kill, so I'm on board with the biological theory. I'm less convinced there are animals from myth gamboling around undetected versus my gene cloning hypothesis. Sell me on it."

"They aren't exactly undetected. Lots of us know about them. They're dangerous in the immediate sense as predators but some have physical features that could be weaponized, in theory. All cryptids also have this ability called the

Chameleon Effect where they blend into their habitat. It's way more real and effective than any stealth technology. It's a predatory adaptation turned up to eleven."

Reading my skepticism, he sighed and kept going. "You're the one who brought up the stuff about myths and monsters. There are plenty of groups who'd exploit that similarity. Get religious with it or use it politically. Seems weird, but people get strange about stuff like that, with prophecies and gods." He shook his head like he was both baffled, and imparting a huge secret.

He hadn't spent time with ultra-religious foster parents, people who subscribed to conspiracy theories, or marginalized rural communities who lived close to their historical roots.

"Assuming I buy that a whole army of people discovered cryptids," his eyes widened in that *oh-shit* twitch again, and I made a mental note, "and individually came to the conclusion they were dangerous, and agreed to keep it on the down-low, *and* somehow kept people who were exposed from blowing the secret wide open, how did you learn about them?"

"I grew up knowing about them."

Yeah, that angelically innocent demeanor probably worked on a lot of people. "How did you learn about what you do, i.e., fighting them?"

A shadow passed over his too-mobile face, hinting at a stubborn roadblock as far as that line of questioning.

I switched tactics. "Somehow, I doubt finding and killing secret animals pays a living wage."

"I'm a personal trainer in my spare time." He propped that ass you could bounce a quarter off of against Sims' desk.

Fine. He looked the part, tall, ripped, and with that outdoorsy tan and perfect white smile. He had the outgoing, upbeat personality necessary to work with the public.

He also had that indefinable air, the one that all law enforcement and career military I'd met had, to one degree or another. The one that said they understood violence, or at least danger, had a mission more than a job, and didn't quite fit in when placed side by side with a normal person.

Three-quarters of the state carried guns, so his being armed while on a midnight beach stroll wasn't noteworthy. The knife he'd whipped out and lodged in the creature's eye certainly was though.

Like my thoughts were in a little balloon over my head for him to read, he challenged, "What do you do in your spare time?"

"I entertain wild ideas from shady men."

He popped upright, indignation coloring his protest. "Hey, I'm not shady."

"That's what you're going to argue about? Really?"

"I'm just putting it out there—I'm one of the good guys." He frowned. "Not good guys as in 'Hey, I'm not a jerk so I deserve a date' but good like not a..."

"Not a criminal?" I hoped not because he had zero game face. He knew something more about me than that I managed an import business. No way was he an undercover officer, nor was he a criminal. He wouldn't have survived this long, hot body and cute grin or not.

His jaw went rigid, even his posture changing, stiffer, an echo of the person who'd attacked and stopped a monster. He wore judgmental like a super hero's cloak.

Fine then. "I don't really care what you think of me, Prescott. All I want are facts. Where is Sims' body?"

"The morgue. Sometimes they get backed up, it takes a while for reports to get posted, and people notified."

"What will his cause of death read?"

"Gunshot. A mugging gone bad, probably." He gave my

middle, where the bellyband holster lived, a significant glare. "You should disappear that gun."

"Because my rounds were in the body. Yet there'll be no mention of evisceration. Want to tell me how you swung that?"

"I'm a friendly guy. I make helpful friends. You should give that a try."

"Did you just try to attitude-shame me?"

"Nah, I succeeded."

He wasn't nearly as amusing as he thought. He might still be useful though. "Species means a population. Are there more of these things in Galveston?"

Panic flashed across his chisel-jawed, team captain face. "Ahh—"

"So there are."

"Ghouls are solitary. We got that one, case closed. It's not like there are packs of them, lurking in the shadows of every city or town."

Which wasn't a no. "If there were more—"

"Which there aren't."

"Where would they go? What's their m.o.? Are they only nocturnal?"

"If there were, which again, there aren't, I'd take care of it. Not you. Understand?"

"Oh, there's that macho bullshit. I can't protect my business because I'm a woman?" His stock took a steep dive, ripped body, dimple, and all.

"What?" His brow furrowed and I braced for an outburst. Possibly one that turned physical. He'd seemed…kind and appealingly laid back, but I'd seen supposedly nice guys turn on people in a heartbeat.

I'd already witnessed his speed and strength. I planted my weight on my left foot, and shook my muscles out.

He cocked his head, watching me, then his expression

changed. He held his hand out, and I backed up a step. He stopped, horror replacing the teasing. "Shit. No, not—I'd do it because I'm trained to take down cryptids, that's all. You're fast and smart. I'm only saying it's a matter of experience." He shoved his hands in his pockets, backing up and giving me space. "I'm not gonna hurt you, McKenna."

"How about educating me, then? Where do they hunt? How do they choose who to hunt?"

He scrubbed a big hand over his face. "You should be fine. Ghouls are primarily scavengers. They prefer the freshly dead or the severely injured and incapacitated."

"Sims was neither."

"In extreme circumstances, they'll go after weak live prey. The one here had to be ill or starving to take on a healthy, armed adult. That was a one-off."

I wasn't sold on him completely believing that. "Supposing I hear of another and need to get in touch with a personal trainer slash cryptid exterminator?"

His jaw firmed up again, lips thinned out.

I got the message. "Forget it. Go personally train some wealthy client with a snowy white background."

"Wait." He reached for me, then checked himself. He grabbed an invoice from Sims' desk, took a pen, and flipped the paper over, writing. He held the finished product out to me. "My number. In case of an emergency. Don't call anyone else, don't talk about it with anyone else."

Grudging help, but it was help. I folded the paper and tucked it in my pocket on the way to the door. I held it open, as ready for him to go as he was to leave. "Bye."

He strode out in a wave of virtuous irritation. Then paused, silhouetted by the afternoon rays, a faceless, imposing shadow. "Ghouls don't like going after healthy prey, but they are vicious as hell if cornered. If you see anything or hear anything odd, don't do whatever you're thinking of—they aren't jokes. And get rid of that Glock."

He pulled the door shut behind him.

Maybe the creatures didn't go after armed adults. That was well and good, unless you were neither.

Say, homeless street kids who were relegated to the fringes, where there was little in the way of police presence, security, or help.

I *wanted* to prove that I wasn't unstable or on Kane's payroll. Get incontrovertible evidence, since Sims' body was now off limits.

I *needed* to make sure Gabbi, Liam, and the other kids weren't going to end up speared on a walking nightmare's claws though.

CHAPTER 5

idge

HAD he just given his number to a civilian, against all Company protocol?

Yes, yes he had.

A criminal civilian at that. A super perceptive, unsettlingly smart criminal civilian.

One who was even more like contained fire and energy up close and in the light of day. Damn, but she was also all soft skin and sleek muscle under her colorful clothes. He'd discovered that when he'd grabbed and broken her fall.

Fire and attitude. McKenna Cabello had nerves of pure steel. She hadn't melted down about the ghoul. Hell, she'd gone looking for either another, or him, rushing toward the problem instead of away. She'd also accepted his word, and asked insightful questions.

Technically, he should report her interest. For most civis

exposed to cryptids, the policy was helping, with mandatory counseling if they'd witnessed or been involved in an attack, relocation and cover story if necessary, and a strict NDA and monitoring. The Company was first and foremost about helping people, the thing he most loved about his life.

Those were average, innocent people

He didn't know the details of protocol for human criminals, other than those assisting cryptids like vampires. Oversight, their ultimate authority, dealt with those.

The Company would undoubtedly tap a human agency they had assets in, or a reciprocal agreement with, to take care of human criminals. Which was justice. He ran his thumb over the scanner at the HQ outer gate, his DNA and prints on file and the security light flashing green. Sets of gates unlocked as he rolled through, then closed behind him.

He parked the car, one of the fleet available for non-mission use, anti-vamp UV lights flaring to blinding levels, then flipping over to plain halogens. Finding the correct slot, he hung the key fob on the garage wall.

Mind still on the civilians, he passed through the long connector between the bays and HQ proper, soft hum of secondary scanners confirming he was all-human, and all-Company.

He left the harsh lights and sterile white and impact proof glass behind, stepping into the central building. He kept going past the junctions leading to cadet barracks, agent suites, classrooms, and Medical, and went left aiming for the Office complex. Ending up at Miguel's door, which was never closed. Alternative rock poured out.

He still rapped on the frame. "You busy?"

"Only the usual. Yo, you missed meatloaf day, and more importantly, Lisle booby trapping Nandi's meatloaf." Miguel pitched his phone at Ridge. "Fortunately, I got video."

Ridge barely glanced at the next stage of the prank wars

between the two surgeons, both from his and Miguel's year group and newly returned from their med school residencies. "Do me a solid and pull up the file on the civilian from my ghoul incident?"

His sibling, in the way all Company members were raised from infancy or toddlers, hit a tab and folded his standing desk into regular format. "Gimme a sec. What are you looking for?"

"Honestly? I don't know."

They'd been trained to trust their instincts though, and keys clicking were the only sounds for several seconds.

"Here." Miguel hooked the chair Josh had pillaged, still not returned to its rightful home. Ridge sat, scanning pages.

The information still read the same. Juvie, petty crimes gradually transitioning to uglier adult activities, LEO surveillance notes. The woman looking out from the photo with a time stamp three years earlier seemed a different version of the one he'd sparred with. It wasn't simply that her hair was longer in the mug shot and not tipped in flaming hues.

Here, those arresting brown eyes held something. Stupid to say innocence, because even past McKenna had the same guarded expression. Maybe something that more resembled satisfaction. Like even in a mug shot, she'd achieved a goal.

For all Ridge knew, getting busted was some sort of street crime rite of passage.

This time, he paid more attention to the reports. Her apartment was in the older center of town. Not the area with new high rises and boutiques he'd half expected, but closer to the edge where gentrification hadn't quite made inroads yet. He'd hit the neighborhoods on several missions when this area's team was rotating to secondary bases in their patrol Region, or for training exercises with past cadets.

All Company members had a shaky grasp on things

financial like salaries and home costs and bills. They had everything—food, education, housing, medical needs—provided from infancy. Technically, they got a salary but it was for whatever hobbies or fun they wanted. Concerts and memorabilia in Miguel's case, band photos and posters all over his suite, and a few hung here in his workspace.

Outdoor and surf toys for Ridge, a natural to go with the personal trainer cover he gave civilians.

He did understand McKenna's Jeep was new, the building she worked from modern. He also recognized her clothes were expensive, like music video stars' styles, thanks to growing up with Vee and her obsession with civilian culture.

There were too many disconnects with McKenna—brave, concerned enough to examine a stranger to make sure he wasn't injured. But also someone who helped sell weapons to the highest bidders, like drug cartels and terrorists. She was willing to physically punish those who opposed her boss. Someone with expensive tastes but living in an area people seemed to leave when money allowed.

For the first time, he wondered about a civilian. Whether she'd had parents once, or whether she was like them, no parents or had never known them, and whether she cared. When she'd chosen to turn her back on rules. Why she was all he'd been able to think about for the last twenty hours. Just…why.

He heard himself saying, "Can you go deeper?"

Miguel blinked at him. "Deeper. On a civilian? You?"

Ridge fiddled with one of the bobble-head musician figures on the desk. "Humor me."

"When have I not? At least this one won't involve stealing cooking spray, and the outdoor course's scaling wall."

"Yeah, scrubbing the whole course down with tooth-brushes until nothing was slippery was not a good ROI. Although—"

"Josh and Jace on their asses," they said at the same time, and tapped knuckles. "You do have stellar ideas." Miguel angled the screen toward Ridge again. "Dead end."

They both stared at the classified emblem centered over McKenna Cabello's photo, where there should've been records containing more of her background and details of her current life.

"What does that mean?" Ridge leaned, nose nearly touching the ominous red lettering.

"I don't know for certain. It requires level six clearance, and I'm only level four. Not all of us are Company stars like you and get to skip the ranks so quickly."

Ridge frowned, but his friend's face was open and earnest, no sarcasm visible. "I'm an instructor. Not a C.O. like Vee, or even a team member."

Miguel paused, hands over the keyboard. "You made Instructor straight out of Academy."

Like Ridge had missed that harsh fact. Miguel had been an intel guy since he learned the alphabet though. He'd never been on the field team track. Not the guy's fault he didn't grasp the nuances. "Got any guesses what the block on her file means?"

Miguel shrugged. "Given her priors and current position in an arm's dealers crew, my bet would be a lockdown from Homeland or the CIA. She's under some kind of surveillance and not in a good way. Once they decide to move on a target, the CIA subscribes to the scorched earth policy. That problem will take care of itself," he added, hitting a key and the screen going dark.

* * *

Despite rereading the sections of her file available and seeing firsthand the shit she was involved in, Ridge couldn't shake the thing, the inexplicable surge of horror at thinking of McKenna in some secret prison.

It had to be the concept of any human getting violently cut down or tortured. Both were anathema to Company code.

That had to be it. Pure training kicking in, no other motive.

He told himself that all evening. Through updating his syllabus and double-checking notes he'd already memorized on his incoming class.

Which explained exactly nothing as to why he found himself parked outside the address listed as McKenna's home twenty-four hours later.

He'd already visited her workplace, and found it closed, following the nine to five receiving hours listed on the front door.

He was reasonably sure in the civilian world his actions were defined as stalking. The fact that there was a cryptid-based qualifier might excuse his choices.

Or not, since the shiny orange Jeep was parked in front of her home, meaning she was safe inside instead of out walking into a cryptid's hunting grounds as he'd feared.

Saving McKenna from a ghoul didn't give him the right to replace a cryptid threat with what would look to her like a human one. His maybe-paranoia wasn't justification for frightening her or causing her to feel unsafe.

As the sun shifted to the west, he put the car in gear, checking his mirrors for pedestrians. Instead, he caught McKenna's image. She came out of the modest duplex, locking the door then double-checking her work.

She tapped a message on her phone, staring at the screen. After a beat, a frown creased her forehead, visible even from across the street. She hit a button, holding the phone to her ear.

Whoever she was trying to reach clearly wasn't cooperating. Her frown deepened. When she shoved her phone into the pocket of her wide-legged pants, her half-jacket, half-sweater thing swung and Ridge got an eyeful of shoulder holster.

The only reason someone who typically used a bellyband version like he'd noticed before would switch to the bulkier shoulder holster involved weapon size. Say, they'd switched out the smaller Glock for a larger forty-five with more stopping power because they intended to go looking for something they already knew wasn't susceptible to smaller rounds.

Ridge swore and slapped the steering wheel.

HQ said let it go, that the chance of another ghoul inhabiting the same territory was minimal. Theoretically, so was the likelihood of the same witness ever crossing paths with one again even if there was another of the solitary predators here.

But Vee's concern, and the two ghouls in one day and only miles apart, sat fresh in his mind. Added to that was his witness, who'd now significantly upped her firepower, seemingly out of the blue.

Every fiber in his body shouted it wasn't a coincidence and she hadn't simply taken his advice, abandoning the gun that implicated her in a murder and randomly chosen a larger weapon as its replacement.

She was set on a course that had a decent chance of ending with her as another cryptid statistic.

Criminal record or not, the Company was tasked with saving any human from that fate.

As his personal mission grabbed an eye-searing pink and green backpack from behind the driver's seat and moved down the street on foot, he turned his car off and locked it.

He kept what he hoped was a realistic distance behind her

as the terrain turned from small duplexes and the occasional boutique and chain restaurant, to tienditas, local shops, and apartments with bars on the windows. The part of Galveston tourists didn't see.

Here, his quarry stopped to talk to people on the street, to people who hailed her, to shop owners. The sudden side-forays kept Ridge on his toes.

She paused after speaking to an older lady, one he assumed was a street person from the shopping cart piled with a sleeping bag and water jugs instead of purchases. Ridge darted into a shop door a millisecond before McKenna turned his way.

The roar of dryers and the ammonia of what he guessed was hair color met him. The glares of several annoyed older women had Ridge apologizing and retreating out of the small salon.

The flame tips of McKenna's hair disappeared around a corner, and he hustled to catch up.

He arrived in time to watch her slide through a split in a chain link fence, and head to the back door of a boarded up apartment building.

When she put fingers to her lips and blew a shrill blast, following it with pounding out some complicated pattern on a plywood window, he jumped like a first year cadet. Then ducked into the shadow of a billboard as McKenna grabbed what turned out to be a rusty folding chair, popped it open, and sat with her back to the building wall. She dropped the backpack on the weedy ground beside her.

A moment later a couple of people came out, circling McKenna.

Shit. Two kids, not adults as he'd expected. These looked younger than the second year cadets, one in multi-colored twists, the other with half their head shaved, the opposite side a neon-red wave. A third, a boy, stuck his head out, then decided it was either safe or interesting and joined in.

After a few minutes of conversation he couldn't make out, McKenna nudged the backpack toward the girl with the twists.

Ridge's stomach churned. Was she using kids to move weapons or cash? Although the bag wasn't big enough for much.

The girl glanced inside and held her hand out. She and McKenna gave an intricate high-five-shake. The girl passed the bag to her friend but the boy intercepted, tossing it hand-to-hand over his head, clearly teasing.

The bag must not have completely zipped after the girl looked inside. Familiar white bars of soap tumbled out, along with a bottle of shampoo, a box of tampons, what he was pretty sure were gummie candies, and another bottle with a label the same intense fuchsia as the second kid's hair. All fell on top of the boy's head. He yelped at the rain of feminine products and tossed the bag at the others.

McKenna's laugh carried, as unexpected as her earlier whistle, and she bent, helping repack what sure as hell looked like a bag of basic provisions.

Before Ridge could process, like it was choreographed, McKenna darted from the chair, and around the opposite side of the building. The kids retreated back inside. The door slammed, echoing across the empty yard.

"Shit." He stepped out, trying to decide—cut through the yard, in plain view, or run the longer way down the block and hope he didn't lose McKenna at the intersection.

The thump of boots hitting dirt behind him answered his question.

He spun, hand on knife hilt. And came face to face with McKenna.

Her swingy jacket was tucked behind the holster on her left side. Giving him a purposeful view of her gun. At least her arms were safely crossed, though the narrow-eyed glare she directed at the center of his forehead wasn't exactly what he'd call welcoming.

CHAPTER 6

McKenna

"I HOPE you're more stealthy when stalking cryptids, Prescott." I rested against the chain-link, this section sturdy enough.

His face went scarlet under his tan. "Stalking is…a very strong word."

"Strong, yet apt."

He looked up and I caught the moment he located the path I'd taken to reach him. A fire escape at the edge of Gabbi's safehouse, then across a section of fence now scaffolded by two-by-fours, coming out where it braced against the untended billboard. The wood all came from scavenging various storm-destroyed houses.

The setup was the kids' secret entrance and exit when avoiding anyone they needed escape from—cops, gangs, other street kids, the rare social worker or parent.

In my case, an inexplicably nosy cryptid hunter who was

hiding plenty of secrets, and who stood out, all preppy blond surfer-guy in a primarily non-Anglo, blue collar area.

"Smart." He eyed the walkway. "Did you build it?"

"The kids are plenty intelligent and resourceful enough to have implemented a safety route on their own." Although the smartest of them was MIA.

Gabbi hadn't answered texts or calls in the last eighteen hours. Now I knew her crew hadn't seen or heard from her either. A hard knot sat somewhere between my heart and gut. Gabbi might be pissed at me and my lack of progress in locating Liam. I was pissed at myself. But she'd never bail on her household.

Yet she seemingly had and I needed to find out why. "Bye, Prescott."

"Why the new accessory?" He tilted his head, eyes fastened on my holster and leaving no doubt what he meant.

"You didn't care for the old one." Which sounded like I cared and worse, like I was flirting.

That annoying dimple came to life. "So you did pay attention."

"I didn't so much pay attention as was unable to overlook you, smack in my space." Which sounded even flirtier.

I didn't flirt when I was into a guy, and this one was wasn't my type. At least, not anymore. After Ryan, too blond, too self-righteous, and too wholesome were on my no-fly list. Permanently.

Ridge's grin grew.

"I switched out calibers because there may or may not be an entire world I knew nothing about, and there may or may not be another predatory entity in *my* territory." Facts were the only antidote to my banging on the bureau therapist's door and giving Freidricks ammunition for his argument to jerk me out and bench me. I needed to be in motion, and in control.

I'd spent the hours I wasn't on the street digging into cold cases. Specifically, cases with weird stamped all over them. Included prominently were those citing animal attacks within city limits, when the worst we had to worry about were coyotes and that one stray cobra that escaped some idiot owner.

It turned out there were a lot of suspect deaths when you used the right search parameters.

So I was willing to believe my eyes, the evidence, and to a lesser extent, Mister Personal Trainer Moonlighting As A Cryptid Expert.

"I told you, leave that to me," Ridge said.

"You're only one person, and this is a large city. My part of it? We are accustomed to taking care of ourselves because we are low on anyone else's priority list." I skirted him, ready to find Gabbi and Liam.

"McKenna—"

I whirled on him and he backed up. "Tell me to my face, and I mean look me in the eye when you say it, that there's zero threat. That the residents of this neighborhood, and those kids, have nothing to fear. Tell me you're only here because you want authentic al pastor tacos."

His jaw worked. Then he did the one thing that surprised me. Aqua blue eyes met mine. "Cryptids are animals, meaning they have consistent, instinctive behaviors. Like I said, ghouls usually prefer the dead, especially when there's no embalming and chemicals, those close to death, and the seriously ill or wounded. The helpless."

I chewed on that for a minute. "Cemeteries, of course. Anywhere there's a homeless population." A terrifying possibility hit and that rock-hard worry in my chest grew. "Do they hang out around playgrounds? Hospitals, or nursing homes and clinics?"

His smile had vanished, but a weird expression lightened

his face. "Yes to the first. We—I—do a fair amount of patrolling where there are homeless, especially if there's alcohol or drugs to complicate the situation. No on medical facilities or any place with high traffic. They're primarily nocturnal." He scowled. "Usually."

"True or false. Killing them requires either a huge caliber and luck, or something that will penetrate their hide, or a kill shot to the brain, through the eye or underjaw like alligators." I waited for his answer.

"Damn. Alligators?"

"I spent time in Louisiana with a family who hunted them during the season. Gator skin is tough." I flicked a finger at him, taking in his abraded arm and leg. "Did you clean those?"

He raised his arm and checked out the scabbed length like he'd never seen it before. "Sure. This wasn't a big deal. Ghoul skin is more like shark skin than anything reptilian—rough and sharp at the same time."

I stared at him. "Sharks?"

"Hey, you have alligator experience, I have shark. Surfing hazard," he said.

Of course he surfed. And I was most certainly not suddenly picturing him in nothing but board shorts. "You are a walking, talking stereotype."

"Uh—is that bad?"

Anyone else and I'd have called the blank look and accompanying confusion pure acting. With Prescott, it seemed as real as his blond roots.

I borrowed a phrase of Gabbi's. "I can't with you."

"Okay?"

"Continuing our cryptid one-o-one course, blades of suitable length, and rounds to the eye. Nocturnal, avoids crowds and noise, prefer incapacitated prey, except when they don't. Got it." I twitched, settling the open-weave summer cardigan, the lightest cover to be had, back over my piece. Open carry was legal, but around here, exposed holsters signaled a war brewing. I wasn't having businesses close early and people lose a day's pay for no reason.

I strode in the direction of the free clinic, my destination before I'd spotted my groupie.

The one who was by my side again immediately, his longer legs catching up easily. "That's all accurate, but there's more to stopping ghouls."

"Fast, teeth and claws, smart enough to attempt passing as human in low light, aggressive with food and when cornered. Got all that on my own. You're off the hook. I take complete responsibility for my actions henceforth."

"Did you see another one?" He cut in front of me.

As if a human speed bump would stop me. "No." I swerved around him.

"You'll call me if you do?"

"Doubtful." Since he'd only grudgingly given me his number.

"You'll ask your people, then." He made it a statement as he caught up with me.

The task force that already suspected I was dirty, and looking for ways to derail the operation, or the even more cut-throat Renee Kane, who had his own questions about one of his favorite general's demise. Kane, whose method of dealing with a potentially unstable member was shoot, shovel, and shut up.

I huffed a brittle laugh. "I don't have people."

He cut in front of me again, but kept walking. Backwards. "The guy with you at your business? The others you deal with?"

I didn't imagine his incredulity, or the way he hit *deal with,* giving it judge-y undertones. I added sanctimonious to his list of flaws. Sanctimonious cancelled out half-naked in board shorts. "You are going to walk into a trash can, food cart, or angry bystander, and bust your head open. There's no one I'd trust at my back, especially with a semi-sentient animal that looks like a cranky abuelita's bedtime story for naughty kids."

Pure sadness crept over his face.

Despite my dire prediction about his head, I was the one stumbling.

Prescott caught my arm, his forehead scrunched in concern. "Hey, steady. I got you."

"I caught my shoe on a crack." I was sticking with that story. Certainly not that his transparent concern had thrown me. Again.

Nor was I acknowledging that I removed my elbow from his grip gently, as opposed to shoving him off in the manner I would anyone else. Needing an assist or acting with kindness was viewed as weakness, from either side of my split life.

"So, you aren't going after a ghoul. Now look me in the eye and say that," he said, stealing my earlier line.

I was an undercover agent. The last years of my life were an ongoing lie. I was a pro at lying believably to people's faces.

Which did not explain why, "I'm not not-hunting them," came out of my mouth.

He finally fell in beside me, sparing me any more of his weirdly intense scrutiny. "Right. You don't have anybody, and you're not not-hunting. Where are we going?"

"Excuse me?"

"You don't have help. I'm here, and I'll be your team. Your backup. We'll work together." He sounded…pleased didn't begin to cover it. More akin to someone scratching off a lottery ticket and discovering they'd won

"A, I don't have backup because I don't require any, and B, even if I did, I don't know you."

"That's fair. The last part, about not knowing me, not the first. A team's always better." He waved my objection off. Like, literally waved a big, scarred hand. "You know I surf. I'm a good shot. Excellent, really," he said with no bragging, like it was a simple fact. "Great in a crisis, and I'm your go-to for cryptid facts."

"And a personal trainer." If there was one way to get rid of someone, it was poking at their cover story.

I believed he was a trainer—but that wasn't the extent of his life. It wasn't what defined him.

"Right. A pretty good personal trainer," he got out a beat too late. "My turn."

"Pardon?"

"You're learning about me, I'm learning about you." He made a back and forth motion. "Exchanging stories, team building."

"Are you for real?"

He blinked those thick-lashed eyes, practically exuding sincerity. "Sure. You had a lot of foster families, besides the alligator one and the exorcism one."

My hand was on my gun before his question died away, pure reflex since I'd already established Ridge had viewed the public version of my files. I was already positive he wasn't a rival or Kane's spy. I tried playing my jumpy reaction off as straightening my shirt.

He tracked my every twitch though. Ridge held both hands out at waist level, palms up and empty. His voice lowered and fell into a soothing cadence. The method you used on terrified civilians, cornered criminals, or talking a jumper down. "I checked into your background a little more, okay?"

"How?" I doubted he'd give me the complete truth, but I also understood how to chip away at other people's secrets.

"Same as hiding what happened to your business partner. I told you, I'm a friendly guy. You already know I'm not the only person who handles cryptids. We've got a network of contacts. People we've helped. I had to know if you were going to need help, too. You were cool during the fight, but once that adrenalin fades and there's time to think, it can mess with people."

He tipped his head back, staring at the sky. "I also needed to know if you were going to try using what you'd learned for not so great ends. None of this is a surprise, McKenna."

I didn't know if it was his factual recital, the familiar method he handled the situation, identical to what I'd learned in the academy—or even the way he said my name. Possibly all of those, plus the way people had given us our own bubble, crossing to the other side of the street. Wary gazes darting to me, then away.

I drew in a deep breath of grilling food, sunbaked concrete, and car exhaust. Exhaled and took my hand from under my knit shrug. "Fine. I'll buy what you're selling. You've already learned I have a record. Aren't you worried I'll leverage this cryptid revelation for—what was it? Not so great ends?"

He became engrossed in staring at the toe of his sneakers —name brand but basic, nowhere near my sneakerhead game —then met my gaze. "I hope you won't. I don't know why you do what you do, but I do know you jumped in trying to save your friend, then again with me."

"I could've simply been thinking of my business or myself. Purely selfish motivations."

"I don't think that's true."

"Based on?"

"Instinct. You aren't a bad person."

I blinked against what was definitely not tears, instead fumbling shades out and slapping them on. Had to be the sun making my eyes water. I was not melting into an emo puddle because someone assumed the best about me. No matter how long it had been since anyone hadn't jumped to harsh conclusions first. "You're undoubtedly a terrible judge of people."

"Nah, I'm terrific at it. You're not a hopeless bad guy." Like he felt the mood and understood I needed to lighten it, he flashed that killer smile. "I have many mad skills."

"You're one of *those*."

"One of what?" He edged close, as if he honestly couldn't wait to hear what I had to say.

"An optimist. Perpetually cheery."

"Those aren't bad things."

"A cupcake. You are a human cupcake."

"Hey, people looove cupcakes. They're *awesome*."

This guy. "A cupcake with freaking sprinkles. Not even plain sprinkles, which are bad enough, but the glittery ones. You are six feet of glitter-sprinkle covered cupcake."

"Six-one. Glitter sprinkles are also awesome, especially the really sugary ones. You know, the extra festive kind? People looove rainbow sprinkles too, Mac."

He had *not* just given me a nickname. Nor had he given me a visual of licking icing off him and his poorly concealed abs. Clouds were obscuring the sun but it felt like the temperature had spiked in the last few seconds. "Sugar causes cavities. And diabetes."

Arriving at my destination, the free clinic, saved me. "Stay put," I said, over the protest already forming on his lips. "They know me. They don't know you and are less likely to talk to me if you're standing over me. You exude authority figure vibes, and this is so not your audience."

His expression cleared and he gave me a nod, retreating across the street to a food truck.

Prescott was a fancy, glitter decorated cupcake who used his head, and respected my opinion. It was unnerving.

I joined the small group outside, hoping someone had seen or had news about Gabbi or Liam.

After my usual hour, I had useful reports on territory disputes, new arrivals, requests couched in mostly non-binding language because they knew I'd help without requiring payback, but nothing else on Gabbi.

I left the purposeful hubbub of the clinic, blinking against the sun. On some level, expecting my new shadow to have bailed on me.

When an increasingly familiar wide shouldered form stood from one of the tables by the food truck, I wasn't sure if I was disappointed or pleased. I couldn't remember the last time anyone had kept their word to me when it didn't involve a direct benefit to them.

I met Prescott as he wound through the maze of tables.

He handed me a bag and a soda, same logo as the cup he reached back and picked up from his table.

I peered inside the bag—two of the truck's monster burritos. I had a policy of not accepting food or drink I hadn't seen prepared.

But the hopeful cupcake in human form in front of me...I couldn't bring myself to erase his smile, even as I resisted the lure of smoky pork and the sharp tang of tomatillo.

Carm, the truck owner who knew me and my quirks, poked her head out of the serving window. "He hasn't touched the food since I handed it to him—it's clean. The ice has probably melted in your drink though. Deberías hacer un mejor trabajo entrenando a tu nuevo juguete sexual."

"¡Dios mío, Carm!" I prayed watered down soda was the

worst I had to deal with, and that Prescott's Spanish was rudimentary.

"You bring many badly trained boy-toys here?" His smile was slow and wicked.

Heat flooded my face. So much for crappy Spanish. "Do I look like I need two burritos?" I executed the clumsiest topic change in the history of embarrassed women as he gave Carm a cheery salute.

"Nah." He reached into the bag, sun-warm skin brushing mine. "FYI, I do like al pastor."

I kept myself from scrubbing at my goosebumpy skin, refusing to draw attention to my reaction to a simple touch from Prescott.

He peeled foil off the burrito, taking a healthy bite, and then groaned in ecstasy.

My skin went nuclear. I took a sip of soda to cool off. "You also like orange soda?"

"Senõra Carmella told me to get it because it's your favorite. You have a lot of friends."

I bit into tender pork and the heat of chilis, chewed, then washed it down. I wasn't sure when I'd last eaten and his reaction to Carm's food was justified. "You're basing this on what? One vendor interaction? I'm a good customer, a source of cash."

"She knew your favorite. Sure, that might be business. I'd already paid though, so there was no reason for her to make the extra effort in telling you I hadn't messed with your food, except friendship." He ducked his head. "I didn't think about caution in taking food from me or how my giving it to you might read. Sorry."

I bit down on the out of character reassurance itching to come out of my mouth, promising him that I didn't believe he'd drug anyone's drink, and went with, "One interaction isn't conclusive. Thank you. I was starving."

"You're welcome. I also saw how all those people at the health clinic were comfortable talking with you. Especially the teens. Nice envelope you slipped the reception nurse on the way out."

Ridge Prescott was too attentive for his own good. Definitely for my own good. From behind my drink, I blew his praise off. "Community good will and all."

"Why were so many people there today?"

"Today isn't only medical care. One day a week, the clinic passes out supplies until they run out."

"Supplies maybe partially funded by stealthily passed envelopes," Ridge said, that strange pleasure coating his words. "Guess I'm not the only one who needs to work on their ninja-secretive skills."

This, this having someone assume the best of me, it was messing with me. Time for a topic shift. "How did you not only learn about cryptids but how to do what you do in eliminating them?"

"Why did you give a backpack of shampoo and stuff to those kids?" He lifted a shoulder in a charming *what can you do* gesture. "A secret for a secret, McKenna. I'll start. I had good teachers, people who also monitor cryptids and help defend people. Those of us who know make it a point to pass on what we've learned—lore, techniques, all of that."

"You've trained people, too?"

"Yes. That was two secrets. Your turn."

"I never explicitly agreed to your plan."

"You'll tell me. You aren't a cheater." He said it the same way you'd say grass is green, an irrefutable fact.

"The house is sort of run by a friend. She has rules for the others that stay there. I help out when I can, especially with items in short supply at the clinic or shelter."

"Gummies and hair dye?"

"Gummie vitamins. Their diet isn't exactly full of leafy

green vegetables and fresh milk and they're kids, who'd toss those gross, chalky vitamins out in a hot minute." I searched for the words to get him to understand. "The hair color is because—why not? There should be more to life than just surviving."

"I don't have parents. Kind of like those kids don't."

I jerked to a halt and my overfilled burrito slid, threatening to hit the ground.

He grabbed and caught my meal, hand wrapped around mine. "I didn't say that right, did I? I meant that I wasn't raised with parents."

There was every chance he was playing me. He'd seen at least part of my file the task force created, all but the juvie and arrests true. He might be trying to bond over a supposedly shared trauma. "Sorry."

I rationalized my unusual tolerance and kindness—if he was working me, I'd seem to agree and keep him off guard. If by some cosmic coincidence he was telling the truth, then yeah, it sucked. I wasn't knowingly giving the heartless treatment to another orphan.

"I have brothers and sisters," he added. "A whole pack."

"The system let you stay together?"

"The—they wanted us to be close. Have each other's backs, be a family instead of being alone, and have our own insular support network."

Part of me was unreasonably jealous. The other, more clinical part noted another of his micro-hesitations, and the wisp of sadness, there and gone, like a shadow passing over the sun.

There was something going on behind his easy smile and surface-level cupcake sprinkles.

I prodded a bit. "You stayed in touch once you aged out of the system?"

He frowned like he was translating on the fly, then

nodded. "Yeah. We're in the same area, and see each other whenever we have a chance. Some more than others, but at least once or twice a year."

"I was raised in foster care. Never really stayed anywhere long enough to forge those kinds of ties. Although one of the guys from where I stayed for a couple of years—the superstitious foster parent not the gator home, if you're keeping track—and I talk now and then." Despite Carm's all-clear, I would've sworn my tomatillo sauce had been doused with truth serum. My traitorous mouth. Would. Not. Stop. "I guess I do feel a sort of kinship with those kids."

Prescott squeezed my hand, entirely too intimate for a random city street in full public view, his fingers strong and callused but gentle. "Thank you for sharing that with me."

How had a basic afternoon turned into this? Over-sharing. Bonding. Being all too aware that a guy was close enough I caught a hint of coconut-ish sunscreen, and instead of kicking my need for space into high gear, I was at ease.

Comfortable with someone I'd spent a handful of hours with, and who likely had his body weight in secrets.

Like he sensed my limits, Ridge let go and backed off a pace. "What was this afternoon?"

"I already told you that."

"Checking on kids and slipping in some financial assistance, sure. I'm asking about the rest. That phone call and texting where no one answered and your expression when you left the clinic. Then there's the new wardrobe. What else is going on?"

"I hope your car gets towed for illegal parking," I muttered.

He rubbed the back of his neck, but didn't turn the red of a quinceañera dress at getting busted for his sub-par surveillance skills and called out again.

Instead of leaving it as-is, the truth tumbled out. "The kid who is basically the RA for that house? She was concerned earlier this week because one of hers disappeared, and this was a reliable, solid kid. Now I can't get in touch with her and she is the definition of responsible." That insidious worry I'd kept at bay, not looking at it full-on all day, rushed in. "I've hit up all my contacts, and nothing."

"Ghouls are easier to locate at night." Ridge turned toward my place, understanding my thought process and deepest apprehension. "I'll gather gear and meet you at full dark."

"I don't have time to—"

"Even that new piece of yours plus what I'm carrying aren't sufficient for a planned patrol." He talked over my panicky protest. "We got lucky last time. Take a shower, no perfume or anything scented, even deodorant." He cut across the road, opening his car. He paused, calling over its roof, "Full dark. We'll find your kids, Mac."

It was stupid to put any faith in a stranger's promise with time ticking away. Ridge felt more like someone I'd known forever, who I never doubted would have my back and my best interests at heart. Of course, I'd imagined Ryan was trustworthy too, and that had crashed and burned in a spectacular fashion.

There was also a significant chance that I was allowing my raw attraction to Ridge to cloud my judgment.

I still locked my door and dropped clothes and holster on my way to the shower, praying Ridge was true to his word because as of now, he was my best chance at locating Gabbi.

* * *

I SET ASIDE the now cold cup of tea, and slapped the lid of my laptop closed with more attitude than the faithful machine deserved. I'd followed directions, showered and was scented-product free. I'd even foregone conditioner and styling cream, the out of control flyaways tickling my forehead the result.

Grilling my street crew the way a good enforcer should was done. Updating the never-ending progress reports for the task force was also done. I hadn't been able to get into even an episode of my favorite binge-watching go-to.

I was a complete failure at waiting.

Guilt ate at me over sitting here while Gabbi, Liam, and God only knew how many other kids were out there in danger or injured. I checked the time again. Still wondering if I was making a mistake in waiting for Ridge, when I could already be out searching on my own.

Logically, odds were that their disappearance was because of human actions, not cryptid, a situation I was far better suited to investigate. The way Sims' had deflected and danced around the topic when I brought up human trafficking lurked at the front of my brain. Darting out every time I let my guard down, every time I tried concentrating on a project.

The chances were high that I was wasting vital hours sitting on my rear and waiting. Intellectually, I knew that. Ridge had even harped on these ghoul creatures being solitary, and not lurking around every corner.

Yet here I sat, waiting. With little else to do, I probed at the puzzle in my head, examining the emotions and reasoning.

It felt...like I was waiting on the rest of my team to arrive before a mission. Not my crew of street soldiers, either. The real thing, with fellow agents.

Ridge already felt like a partner. Which was ridiculous, as well as stupid. Dangerous, too. Definitely dangerous.

Which didn't stop the fact that I liked him as a person, and trusted him as backup. The revelation was the last straw, and I popped up from the loveseat to find something phys-ical to do—clean, pace, repaint the whole house.

Pounding on my front door, hard enough the wood rattled, halted me.

I hadn't ordered food, one of the two reasons anyone would show up unannounced. The other—Gabbi had never been here, but she and Liam knew where I lived.

I spun to answer, then backtracked to the low table holding my laptop, grabbing my gun. Standing to the side instead of directly in front of the door, where a shooter would aim, I checked my security camera. Zac, one of Kane's junior crew and occasional driver, stood on my stoop. His bulk taking up all the room. Despite the chinos, fashionably ironic tee, and brand new undergrad degree there was a coldness to the guy. As if you looked close enough, you could make out the monster just underneath the human skin.

There was only one reason he'd be cluttering up my porch.

I didn't bother pasting on a smile. That wasn't part of my persona. Nor was laying down the gun first. "Yes?" Opening the door, I addressed the guy but looked over his shoulder, locating one of Kane's business Escalades across the street. Right where Ridge had parked earlier.

"You have a meeting." Zac held his arm out, like he was a host directing me to my seat.

I tucked the gun in my waistband, not an ideal spot, but again, an Enforcer McKenna move. My frustration mixed with the trickle of adrenalin and river of wariness that accompanied spending time in close quarters with the dealer, as I jogged across the road.

When Zac started for the driver's side instead of opening the door for me, I cleared my throat.

He stopped, and turned in slow motion. Face disconcert-ingly expressionless.

I stared him down, not blinking, not twitching toward my weapon.

He broke first, carefully circling around me and holding the back door open. I gave it a beat, before ducking inside.

Kane's chuckle greeted me. "I do appreciate your touch, McKenna."

That he used my first name was a positive sign. "It takes time to properly train the new kids. I don't like making the lessons unpleasant, unless needed." I sank into the air-conditioned comfort, leather *whuffing* as I settled in.

"I agree with your methodology. Why use a heavy hand when a chat is equally useful?" He turned the charismatic force of those blue eyes on me.

Despite being the same shade as Ridge's, Kane's held none of the trainer's openness or joy. There was a surface-level humor. It and the impeccable manners were all curb appeal, though. Meant to draw the unwary or plain stupid inside, where the darkness lurked.

He angled his lean body toward me, ankle over his knee. Still deceptively casual. "As we share that less-is-more mentality in addition to appreciating how much wiser it is to give valued, faithful employees the care they need, I stopped by for a casual chat."

The inside of the car came into hyper focus, my body registering the danger. Kane was excellent at playing the enlightened Millennial businessman. Until he wasn't. "Sir, my crew is in the best shape they've ever been, and we added the new blocks you assigned with no muss, no fuss. I concluded a briefing less than an hour ago."

"I'm aware. I do appreciate the system you've implemented."

"We are making finding information on Sims'— attacker—a priority." I prayed he'd missed the hesitation. "My guys are shaking every tree, and have been quite clear on the repercussions of holding out or sheltering the killer."

"I appreciate that as well. Today is more about you specifically. I feel your focus may be divided."

Part of me froze, like prey sighting a predator. He couldn't know about the task force. He wouldn't have visited in person, or with only one shooter. Ridge though…Markie could've I.D.'ed Ridge as the alleged cop. And Ridge was potentially on his way here, familiar with cryptid dangers but oblivious to humans with weapons.

I felt my way carefully. "I have been out, visible on the streets, and hands-on."

"You've also spent nearly as much time asking questions about missing people."

"Two of my contacts are missing. Potentially more."

His gaze sharpened. "You feel those are related to the attack on Sims?"

I pulled on every bit of skill I possessed, voice calm. "It doesn't seem likely, but I don't think it's wise to ignore any possibility. The contacts were my best."

"And you have a soft spot for them, especially the girl." He relaxed, like a lazy tiger deciding he was too full to bother hunting yet.

I tilted my head in acknowledgement.

"I respect your eye. I have no problem with your setup, or with you grooming and bringing in talent. However, security and Sims' assassination is priority one, indefinitely. I have a slot to fill, McKenna, and several qualified employees vying for it." He held both hands out. "Consider this your annual employee review. I'd hate for you to jeopardize your promotion over a street rat who can be replaced."

"Understood, sir." I pushed down the spurt of rage at his discounting human lives as another commodity, and a cheap one in the kids' case.

"Then I'll consider this a positive interview, and look forward to seeing what you bring me. Have a pleasant night, McKenna."

I dipped my head respectfully, and let myself out of the truck. Zac executed an illegal u-turn, and cruised slowly by me as I walked back to my apartment. Locking the door behind me provided the illusion of safety and privacy, and I half-collapsed, back against the wood.

This could've gone so, so wrong. If Ridge had rolled up mid-discussion, or if Ridge had already been here and answered the door before I could.

Kane was correct in saying my attention was divided. But it wasn't split in half between being his good little enforcer and my finding Gabbi. It was a three-way split—my interconnected jobs, Gabbi, and Ridge. Somehow, he'd made it on my list.

I had to work harder and be smarter so that he wasn't dragged any further into the ugly half of my reality.

idge

RIDGE SMILED and high-fived a couple of agents from the Four Corners Region, in for a HQ pit stop. Not slowing, he waved off a pack of rambunctious second-year cadets motioning him over. "Rain check, yo."

He made it out of the common rooms and aimed straight for the armory. Mentally guestimating McKenna's size—compact, lean, average height—because she wasn't going out tonight without their modified Kevlar.

Today, he'd never been so glad he followed a gut feeling.

The real McKenna was fucking amazing. Smart. Brave. Real. Generous. He'd gotten a longer look under that street enforcer façade. She genuinely cared. Sure as hell about the kids in that hovel, which turned his stomach. Somehow, he was working out means to get all of them someplace that didn't look like it'd collapse on their heads as they slept.

If they ever slept. From the code McKenna used to even

bring them to the door, and the existence of an aerial escape route, he doubted they felt safe enough to really sleep.

The vision of his cadets goofing in the cafeteria superimposed over the teens at the shack, and acid burned up his throat at the contrast between his well-fed, well-cared for, and flat out loved kids, to McKenna's, barely existing on the margins. Where fucking *vitamins* were a luxury.

McKenna cared, and it looked like she was one of the few who bothered.

Given her background, she could've turned callous and cold. Instead, at-risk teens clustered around her, chattering like a favorite sister had arrived. The locals in her neighborhood spoke to her with respect, not the fear he'd expected. He'd gotten an earful from Carm, the food truck owner, as well. McKenna wasn't just a regular, she routinely bought bags at a time weekly, which had to be going to hungry kids.

She'd also gotten Carm's brother into some sort of big deal summer STEM course.

What gunrunner bothered getting a boy into an honor's program, or worried about hair dye for a bunch of street kids?

She worried, period.

He'd felt her fear for the missing girl, stress lines cut deep around Mac's lips.

At the swish of the automatic door opening behind him, Ridge checked over his shoulder. His body kept going through the process of weaponing up on autopilot.

He tightened the thigh holster as he greeted Miguel. "Brother, you are a mind reader. You were my next stop. I need you to pull up that sat map you ran for Vee."

"The ghoul sightings she asked for, before the mission turned into a graduation exercise?"

"Nailed it. Grid a copy and send it to my phone." He'd take their information on sightings, the kills, and previous ghoul dens, and compare with McKenna's knowledge of the neighborhoods and where the kids frequented.

"Gridded. As in, a team's copy for a hot sweep."

"Yeah." Done with his armor, he switched, hitting the general racks. Sorting through the sets most commonly used for female cadets and visiting trainers. He held a vest up—larger than Vee-ish size, smaller than Kimi-ish size, exactly what he needed for McKenna.

"I didn't know there was a patrol scheduled," Miguel said.

"There isn't. I'm feeling antsy. I keep thinking about what Vee said, then today I heard about a couple of missing homeless kids."

"From our contacts? Because again, it hasn't come across my station."

"Nah." Ridge added tactical pants. "Informal info while I was out."

Miguel planted himself in Ridge's path, and slapped a hand on top of the pile Ridge had stacked on a bench, as Ridge grabbed a duffle. "This looks more than antsy. Who's going with you? Mick? Keisha?" His friend tossed out the two instructors who were always willing to hit patrols.

"No. I'm good."

Miguel stared at him like Ridge had proposed bringing in a chupacabra litter as pets. Which, they'd tried once—and only once. Except there was no teasing in his expression. Then he slowly, like he was feeling out a trap, said, "I'll go with you."

Ridge stopped with a set of thigh rigs only partially stuffed into the bag. Miguel was qualified. Everyone from maintenance to medical was. Miguel had also volunteered to patrol or join a call-out for fun exactly never. It wasn't his idea of a party.

"A patrol serious enough that a grid map is required is

serious enough for a two-person team. Minimum. And you have equipment for an additional person."

Ridge should've known Miguel would figure it out.

He also wasn't wrong. Any other time, Ridge would've gathered Mick and Keisha.

But McKenna was involved.

McKenna also wasn't on the right side of the law, and had rabbited from a cryptid scene.

HQ had let it go as her being relatively unimportant and already on human law enforcement's radar.

That live and let live plan might not survive if other agents were presented with a well-armed McKenna in person, a McKenna who clear as day wasn't letting her cryptid discovery go. And odds were good her missing teens were in trouble from human elements, not cryptid. Hopefully, he'd only end up being useful as muscle to impress upon someone that harming kids was no longer on the menu.

"I'm good." He finally met Miguel's eyes. Asking for leniency. "Let it go at that."

Instead, his friend shoved into Ridge's personal space, voice lowered. "Oh, hell no. The only reason I can think of— and I am the creative one who came up with the now legendary gluing of windigo silhouettes to shower stalls on our first overnight cadet exercise—is because of that civilian witness. Tell me I'm wrong."

Ridge had never lied to Miguel. He'd never lied-lied, period. Nobody did. Company was built on that trust.

He was willing to bet his favorite surfboard that McKenna hadn't been brought up that way, and still didn't have anyone she could trust.

So he kept his mouth shut.

"What *the hell*, man? She's not one of us. She isn't even an innocent civi."

"You think I don't know that? I am also telling you, Miguel, my brother and co-mastermind on numerous epic pranks, that she isn't what you think."

Miguel groaned and laced his hands over the top of his head.

Ridge pressed harder. "She looks out for people in her own way, with her own resources. The missing homeless are a couple of kids she's been trying to keep safe. She's already been out looking for them, even aware she could run into another cryptid."

"Then fine. Put together a team and hit it before she gets killed attempting things she isn't qualified for."

"Can you promise she won't get turned over to one of our assets in law enforcement?"

"Ridge, fuck—"

"She had some crap breaks in life, she didn't know better, and we're the last people who should pass out judgment over trying to stay alive. She's never had the support and help we take for granted."

"And you think you'll show her by example. Let her see what's right, and she'll change. Man," Miguel clasped Ridge's shoulder. "She isn't a cadet that will course-correct."

Ridge's slow-to-rise temper flared. "You're wrong, and this conversation is over." He shrugged Miguel's hand off.

"If a couple of meetings with this woman has gotten you this screwed up? You have got to quit." Miguel's equally low-key temper came to life. "You aren't just an agent. You are a damn instructor. *You* are responsible for *our* cadets, and if that doesn't register at the top of your scale of priorities, you need to check yourself and get your head back on straight."

"You done?"

Miguel held his hands out to the side, then turned and left without another word to Ridge.

He and Miguel had never had a true fight where they both walked away still pissed.

Miguel was right that Ridge had a responsibility. But somehow, helping McKenna and kids he'd never met had joined his list of responsibilities.

He was betting everything on being right about McKenna Cabello.

CHAPTER 8

$\mathcal{M}$ cKenna

I HADN'T BEEN a hundred-percent on Ridge living up to his promise, part of me braced for the mother of all disappointments. Not even as his ride, a huge SUV with heavily tinted windows, squeaked into the parking slot beside mine. With anyone other than me, he'd have been wise to put windows down to confirm the driver was a friend, not a rival rolling up. His mirrors were a hair from scrapping the security fence on one side, my passenger door on the other.

He emerged, a duffle large enough to fit a body in slung from his shoulder.

I wasn't conditioned to do the swooning over a heroic Prince Charming thing. However, in a black long-sleeved tee that fit like a second skin, a pair of black tactical pants with thigh holsters over top, and that determined set to his square jaw—I privately conceded he looked the part.

"Hey." He glanced in both directions as he spoke, scouting

91

his surroundings in a way that said the awareness was second nature. The habit did more to seal his competence than weapons ever could, and also lit an inappropriate ember south of my navel.

He stopped at the bottom of my minuscule stoop and the security light haloed him in a golden glow. "Have you heard from your kids?"

They weren't my kids, but at the same time, I couldn't argue the title fit. "Nothing."

"We'll find them." The compassion in his eyes was at odds with the weapons, and scars along his knuckles.

A chunk of my soul ached to believe him, and that we'd be in time. That this situation would have a fairy tale ending. Those weren't real, though, or if they were, they weren't meant for women like me or girls like Gabbi. With Kane's warning, I was surrounded by ticking clocks.

I also wasn't sure I should involve Ridge further in my crisis.

"You brought prezzies?" I said, to kill the moment and the odd, dangerous spark that crackled between us. We needed put back on solid, reliable, friends-only footing.

"I wasn't sure of your measurements but these should work." He held the duffle out, arm the only part of him that ventured closer.

I leaned and took the bag, then grunted and tilted at the unexpected weight, the mass threatening to drag me off the porch.

"Shit, sorry." Ridge grabbed but I'd already adjusted, and our fingers tangled.

Goosebumps raced over my skin again. "I've got it."

Ridge let go like the handles were on fire. "Right. Good." His voice held a husky edge, and he cleared his throat. "There's tactical in there, plus weapons choices."

I slid the zipper a few inches, and discovered why the bag weighed so much.

"You probably don't want to open that out here," he rushed to add.

Since even my quick glimpse registered enough ordnance to take over a small town, I agreed. I hefted the lot inside.

When my front door stayed open, but no Ridge came through, I dumped the load on the table, backtracked, and stuck my head out. "Are you not housebroken?"

"I didn't want to assume. You know, have some guy invite himself in, make you uncomfortable." He shoved his hands in his pockets.

I couldn't remember the last time anyone was concerned with my comfort levels. It felt...weird. So foreign my brain was at a loss trying to process. I scooted back in before anyone saw my cheeks catch fire.

He mounted the stoop in one smooth stride, dwarfing the already small space, and entering.

My place was all open plan, living and kitchen on the first floor, bedroom and bath on the second. I'd put the bag on the largest surface, namely my kitchen table. It was too big for the space, kind of like Ridge, and certainly too much for my one-woman needs.

Unpacking the duffle was deja vu. Too akin to unpacking a sample from one of Kane's shipments.

I laid out a pair of tactical shotguns, what looked like a modified riot gun, the barrel size suggesting it held grenade-style rounds. A Desert Eagle that had to be Ridge's, and a pair of Glocks.

A set of thigh rigs and matching sheaths came next. When I pulled the matching blades free, they proved to be closer to machetes, with an odd silver tint.

At the very bottom—"Is this Kevlar?"

If it was, it was next gen, with what looked like sets for thighs, as well as vests, and some sort of jointed neckpiece.

"Modified Kevlar, smaller pieces, and thinner since what we do is more hand to hand—cryptids are all fast. We can reduce bulk in favor of agility since we're primarily concerned with claws and teeth, not bullets."

Rolled neatly between the sets of body armor was the promised clothing, far smaller than anything Ridge would ever fit in, plus two balaclavas. "Ridge, this is tens of thousands of dollars worth of equipment, even wholesale or black market." I ran my hand along the blades, which also had to be custom work. He'd used *we* when referring to the Kevlar.

"Personal training pays well."

"Ridge."

He grinned. Freaking grinned in the face of my irritation. "You called me Ridge, not Prescott. Twice."

"You are un-freaking-believable." Of course, so was standing in a rental house paid for by a government force as part of a cover story, examining a fortune in high-tech weaponry, while preparing to search for missing teens and potentially fight previously unknown, semi-sentient animals.

I ignored his glee. "I might buy that you have personal weaponry. But how do you explain conveniently having a second set in my size?"

"I'm not sure they're exactly your size. I guessed." His teasing attitude and smile dropped. "This is one of those situations where we're going to have to acknowledge and be okay with both of us having those secrets, Mac."

I tested the weight of the machete-thing, considering my options and Ridge's previous actions at the same time. He seemed genuinely concerned, his face open. I let go of the last suspicions he was going to flake on me when the pressure was on.

"Tell me about this." I nudged the massive shotgun with the tip of the knife.

"It fires incendiary rounds, nothing long-burning." He patted the shotgun, then the Desert Eagle. "Ghouls are one of the cryptids that can venture into well populated areas, which limits the gauge and array of options we can use, but these have adequate stopping power. The Glocks are clean."

He divided the equipment, then pushed the clothing, body armor, gun, and rig my way. He hesitated over the blades. "Are you comfortable with knives?"

I'd enjoyed hand to hand and knife classes in the academy, and had had an unfortunate number of occasions to use the skills since. I settled for a simple, "Yes. Although those are twice the size of anything we carry."

"Show me, with yours." He crossed his arms, biceps testing his shirt's seams.

I pulled a butterfly knife, stupidly flashy, but flash and bluff went almost as far in the organization as skill did.

Ridge tilted his head, checking out my toy, and I feinted for him, aiming for his face. He shifted, as gracefully as with the ghoul. I spun, the small punch blade that magically appeared in his hand a breath from grazing my shoulder.

Retaliating, I swiped for his mid-section. Ducking under his reach and angling hard to one side as he responded, and reaching around his waist. Then flipped the knife, tip pricking over his kidneys as his arms closed around me. The tip of his blade scratching a point on my spine that would've paralyzed me from the pain.

"Good." His praise rumbled like a growl, vibrating through his chest into me where we pressed together. Reminding me of how big he was, easily enveloping me in hard muscles and blocking out the rest of the room.

Carefully, he loosed his hold and set me aside. As if my

getting even an accidental scratch was unacceptable. As careful as he'd been of not violating my boundaries earlier by not automatically inviting himself in.

"You have a sound technique. With cryptids, especially ghouls, remember to go for the eyes and underjaw. They're the only realistic kill shots. You can partially incapacitate by hamstringing, if you hit exactly right."

"Show me."

He took my challenge head on, dropping to one knee, using the hilt of his knife, tapping the inside of my knee, a finger width below the bend. "In the not so distant evolutionary past, they had physiology more like an ungulate so there's still a weak spot. Hit it fast, get clear to leave room for a second strike—"

"If it's a two person tag-team approach," I finished and twirled my knife closed. "Can I?"

He rose, not needing to ask what I meant. "Remember, fast, draw it all the way across because their tendons are twice the diameter of a humans, roll out." He mimed the actions. "Go."

He stomped at me like he was attacking. I hit the floor, rolled, running the covered knife flat across his solid calf. Coming up against the base of my wine cooler, I flipped to my feet, landing in a slightly wobbly crouch.

Respect gleamed in his eyes. "Perfect."

"Good students come from good teachers. I had a top notch teacher."

Shock replaced the respect on his face, and his lips parted. Somehow, I'd surprised him out of a witty reply this time.

He cleared his throat. "You should get geared up."

Far too familiar with awkward-embarrassed changes of subject, I gathered all but the pile of weapons, and climbed the narrow stairs to my equally compact bedroom.

Changing with another person in my house was…different. My hands kept slipping, taking multiple tries to buckle straps and align Velcro. Why I couldn't get fingers to cooperate wasn't important. It couldn't be. Finding Gabbi and Liam was the only thing I had headspace for.

I shoved the odd feelings aside, and boxed them up with all the others undercover agents couldn't indulge.

When I came back down, Ridge was fully dressed. Tall, wide, armed to the teeth, and intimidating as hell. Lethal. Unless you looked deeper, to the laugh lines at the corners of his eyes, and when I met those eyes, to the appreciation sparking in their depths.

"Tactical uniforms suit you," he said, watching as I pulled my hair into a low pony. The same style I'd done when in uniform at the academy.

I was both a woman and had a pulse, so random comments on my appearance were nothing new.

Other people's opinions having any impact on me was though. "They aren't the prevailing style in Galveston. This?" I tapped the surprisingly light vest. "Not inconspicuous."

He pulled out his phone, scrolled and laid it on the table. "I'm thinking where we're going, fashion or reporting heavily armed pedestrians isn't a thing. These are ghoul sightings. Green are past attacks, orange are areas where we've found ghoul dens, and red are the most current attacks."

I joined him and fished my phone out, pulling up a far more generic map of my section of Galveston, then placed it beside his.

They weren't perfect matches, but there were a hell of a lot of green and orange areas that coincided. All of the red ones clustered around me.

"There were *three* other attacks?" A chill worked its way

down my spine. Three of those things, out stalking oblivious people.

"That's why I was at the beach that night."

"How can people not know?"

"Trust me, ghouls at beaches or schools isn't normal. Kinda unprecedented. As for the rest, we make sure they're eliminated, and any evidence disappears."

"We. That's not the first time you've used that pronoun."

He sighed. "I told you there are other people who do what I do, and that we stay in touch. Some of these people are in positions where they can keep cryptids on the down low."

"Don't be coy. Call it what is—suppressing information and keeping the public clueless about a significant threat to their safety." I was displacing, frustrated at myself for not handling the investigation better, for not keeping Gabbi and the kids out of harms way. Scared as hell, because it was easy to replace Sims' face with one of theirs.

Pissed, because of course it was easier to keep information from getting out when so many of the incidents were in poor areas, marginalized communities of one kind or another, with less police presence, fewer cameras, no one to *see* us. It was always the margins that took the worst hits.

"These cryptids are too dangerous, which is the exact reason they need to stay secret. What do you think organized crime would do with ghouls? Windigos? They'd be the next pit bulls, except these cryptids are sentient and see humans as potential meals. Can you envision packs of them loosed on towns as shock troops to soften up resistance by dictators, or groups attempting to overthrow a government? Having that threat in your pocket?" Ridge jerked the duffle close and zipped it hard enough I expected the teeth to break

Then he shoved it away again. We'd ended up on opposite sides of my table and he planted his fists on the top and leaned into my space. "No matter how often you say otherwise, ninety-percent of the people we encounter won't listen when we try explaining that this thing that matches up with monster or demons from some legend are only animals, not supernatural or divine."

I wouldn't be intimidated in my own house. I leaned and met him. "You say *people* you try to explain to. I say *victims* too traumatized to understand."

He swore and scrubbed a hand through his short hair, but I couldn't stop. "What I'm not hearing, but reading between your carefully edited lines, is that you also mean religious people, rural people, and populations with less access to education. The superstitious and ignorant."

"Mac, you've gotta hear me on this." He caught my hand. Okay, my fist, because no, I wouldn't mind punching someone. "That's not what I'm saying. People who are already at a disadvantage are the most vulnerable. I swear to you that those of us who chase cryptids do recognize all those really shitty things, and we show up. We're there, doing every damn thing we know how to in order to protect all these families, and kids, and strangers battling circumstances, and addictions, and illness. I swear."

Cupped between both of his callused hands, mine looked almost delicate. Ridge didn't grab or hold. He cradled mine as if it was an honor, lightly enough I could've taken it back with no effort.

His sincerity wrapped around me like the fading ghost of his cologne earlier, not visible but still real and impactful, a hint of what could've been.

"I believe you try. It's impossible to spend five minutes with you and not believe in your essential Eagle Scout-ness."

"That's a good thing?" His forehead scrunched, and I had a momentary glimpse of kid-Ridge puzzling through an unfamiliar homework problem.

"Yes, it's good. You are one of the few selfless people I know. However, there's only one of you."

"But more like me."

I doubted there were any other people exactly like Ridge Prescott.

"Tonight, there are at least two of us." His smiled chased away some of his sternness. "Ready, partner?"

The term was simply a figure of speech. Ridge couldn't know what it meant to me, and the spurt of …hope, belonging, whatever nebulous emotion he'd accidentally triggered.

I extricated myself, stuffing the feel of his skin on mine, and the odd intimacy, away with the rest of the fantasies boxed in my head. Ridge was testing my ability to compartmentalize emotions to its limit. "The east side of your grid overlaps with most of the kids' bolt holes." I used my elbow to nudge him out, grabbing keys and silencing my phone before securing it in a side pocket.

My neighbors wouldn't be shocked by anyone coming out of my place armed, although this outfit was pushing it. The moonless night covered our sins once we stepped out of the stoop light's glow.

Ridge held his truck door open, sucking and squeezing in even more difficult with weapons added.

I didn't bother hiding my amusement at his antics, and finally said, "Take this exactly how it's meant, but your ride screams *bureaucracy*."

"It's tailored to my needs." He placed a protective hand on the hood like he was shielding it from my insult, his tone indignant.

"I have no doubt. It isn't tailored to inspiring confidence, particularly among street kids. They, and most of my informants, will see a blacked-out SUV, think police, SWAT, or ICE, and go to ground. This excursion is hopefully more about locating people than gunning for cryptids."

He hesitated, tap-tapping his key fob against his palm. "Valid point. There's equipment in here and it wouldn't be good for it to get into regular hands, you feel me?"

"Your ride is safe. As long as it sits in my drive, no one will touch it."

His face settled back into stern planes and sharp edges.

"You have my word."

"I wasn't doubting you." He torqued his body into all kinds of painful looking angles, and managed to squash into the side door and fish around in the back. A soft click sounded, then a second, and he wiggled out butt first. He straightened, holding his prize.

The red and white emblem was the same, but I'd never seen a first aid kit this big, other than on an ambulance.

"Do you know how to use everything in that pack?" I slid behind the wheel.

Ridge secured the kit in the back, then dropped water bottles on top, before climbing in. "You can't do what controlling cryptids requires without an intimate knowledge of field medicine."

Catching my stare, he snapped his seatbelt closed. "A good number of us have EMT training."

I put the Jeep in gear, thinking his matter of fact comment over. EMT made sense. They were the people at every medical emergency, accident, or violent crime scene. There had to be a generous overlap—they'd frequent the same places ghouls preferred. Someone with the fortitude to ride an ambulance would also have the temperament for what Ridge did. "Let's pray we don't need to put your skills to use."

* * *

THREE HOURS INTO OUR SEARCH, and all we had to show for the night was sweat-soaked clothing and the mounting sense of a timer on a countdown.

I'd memorized the statistics on missing people, especially those homeless and under eighteen. We were already on the downward probability curve of this having a good outcome.

For all I knew, it had been too late before I even realized Gabbi wasn't answering my texts or calls.

I rested against a wall, the wood more spongy than solid. A remnant of the last major hurricane, abandoned when the owners couldn't afford repairs, left to disintegrate in on itself. Tilting my head back and ponytail acting as a cushion, I stared at the past-midnight sky. Clouds obscured the stars, while the wet dog stink of mold worked its way even deeper into my pores.

"Hydrate." Rough fingers gently opened my limp hand, then wrapped it around a water bottle.

Our last, which he was offering me. Because over the course of the evening, I'd learned that was simply who Ridge was.

People talked to me because they knew me, and recognized one of their own. But a few minutes around Ridge, and they spoke as readily to him.

He'd cleaned and bandaged a regular's burned arm, leaving the burn cream and the remainder of the roll of tape and pads, all while engaging in gun talk with a younger military veteran. I'd also seen him slip cards for a shelter that had a job program and therapists to a couple of newbies to the street. It was a place I'd have suggested if it wasn't always full. I hoped these two took his advice.

Ridge wiggled my hand, reminding me of the water.

"You first. " I attempted to hand the bottle back. "I'll take whatever's left over. I'm confident ultra-competent, shredded personal trainers are ridiculously health conscious, so even your saliva is undoubtedly organic, vegan, and germ free."

"Mac?" Those same strong fingers whispered over my cheek. "You okay in there?"

"Drink the damn water. Please." I let go of the bottle, which Ridge presumably rescued before it hit the ground, judging from the crack of a seal breaking a moment later, and the soft glug of liquid.

I ground the heels of my hands into my gritty eyes. Then got my shit together. "Right. We've exhausted all Gabbi and Liam's bolt holes that I'm aware of, and every encampment and contact out here." Plus all the sites of recent attacks. I forced out the words I hadn't wanted to have reason to utter. "Where's the first den thingy around here where a ghoul would take its dinner?"

"Finish this. Cause it's true. Personal trainers are hella organic and ick-free." He poked me in the stomach with the bottle. "I'm not allowed to *officially* say this water is purer than when it came out of—" he quit poking to bring the bottle closer, squinting at the label "—when it came out of an Adirondack mountain stream, buuuut, yeah, it is. That's just one of my super powers."

"There's nothing worse than a guy who thinks he's funny." A grin still snuck up on me.

"Except, I am a comic genius." He waggled the water that in all likelihood came from a tap and purifier in some manky factory, eyebrows jumping up and down.

As I accepted and drained the last—he'd left at least half —Ridge tested leaning back on the wall. When it didn't buckle, he committed, his shoulder bumping mine and staying.

He rested quietly, offering his silent support. I had to assume he'd worked with others, and often. The extra equipment aside, he seemed to grasp when there was nothing anyone could say that would help an ugly truth, and how to let people process.

Any contact when it was humid enough to see a misty haze should've been intolerable. The warmth of his arm and shoulder was as soothing as it was weird. Giving me a brief time-out, an offer to take part of my burden momentarily.

When I capped the bottle, he took the empty, tucking it back into one of his pockets. He refused to litter, even here where wind and rain blown trash piled in gutters and long-ruined buildings, ribbons of blue nylon from shredded tarps that had once covered damaged roofs twining along trees and weeds like colorful spider webs.

"Ready?" He straightened and when I nodded, produced his phone, offering me the map. I took it and he pulled out the throat and neck guards we hadn't put on earlier, handing me mine.

The way he shared, let both of us do what we excelled at, felt like the kind of partnership I'd imagined police work was when I signed onto the task force.

I got back to reality, matching our current location to those nearest Gabbi's routes. "Here." I traced along, finger an inch above the screen.

"That's—a school?"

"It used to be. Despite it being newish, repeated floods were too much. It was easier to shuffle attendance to schools that weathered the flooding better than to redo or rebuild."

Ironic as hell that Gabbi and her friends used the spot to party.

Without any outward signal, we moved on. Ridge watched every shadow, every nook, tree, or building outline. The funny, laidback surfer was gone, leaving a professional soldier in its place.

Where he'd been alert with that innate awareness all military and police developed while we were among people, fraught as the homeless camps and underpasses could be, now he was contained focus.

He flowed from shadow to shadow, eerily silent. As at home as if he was something other than human, too. The shotgun was pulled around on its sling, an extension of his hand, finger off but alongside the trigger.

We moved block-by-block, working beside each other, quartering the area before moving on.

The closer we got to the school, the louder the ticking in my head became.

The school was set up like a wheel. The main building was at the center, and four individual buildings at each compass point. The outbuildings were attached by covered walkways.

We approached across the sport's field, the chain link fence that once protected children torn and leaning. One section had been ripped completely free, posts jerked out of the ground, the concrete that had anchored them still around their bases.

The storms had been serious, category three or four. Like tornados, hurricanes could do strange things, leave one house standing, another destroyed down to the pilings. Still…something was off.

Brighter silver glinted under the post's layer of grime. I stopped, studying the distracting section of fence. Peering closer, the shine turned out to be parallel lines, the gunk scrapped off so that raw metal showed.

Ridge turned, and not finding me behind him, hustled back. Instead of arguing or ordering me forward, he stood beside me, focusing where all my attention was. He laid his fingers over the gouges, then traced the five perfectly spaced grooves.

Hairs rose along my arms, my body understanding the danger before my brain caught up. Claw marks.

Something had grabbed an entire section of heavy-duty fencing and concreted posts and ripped it free.

Ridge put a finger to his lips in warning. I didn't need the order. My mouth went dry enough that my tongue felt cemented in place.

He knelt, studying the ground. When he stood, he signaled me to stay, making a short arc in front, focused on the terrain at his feet.

He returned and bent, lips brushing my ear and bringing on a whole body shiver. "A ghoul is using this as its entry and exit point. A fairly large one, adult male."

I nodded and he continued. "I'll take point. You watch our backs." He touched my Kevlar collar, testing that I'd fastened it properly. I scrubbed damp palms on my pants, then holstered the Glock with its decidedly non-LEO compliant forty-five rounds. I inhaled, held it, exhaled, slowing my runaway pulse, and pulled the shotgun around.

I took my spot, trusting that Ridge read whatever tracks or spoor correctly and he knew what he was doing by choosing to start with the eastern building, the one furthest from us.

An endless expanse of wide-open field lay between us and the building.

Sweat owing more to fear than temperature dotted my forehead and gathered along my waistband. My senses felt stripped bare, every whisper of air against my face, every tickle of weed against my pants either giving us away or heralding a creature charging out of the dark at us as we slunk across the open ground.

A million heartbeats later, we made it to the twin aluminum trailers serving as the first classroom. The door had long ago been torn loose. Ridge went in low, sweeping the cramped area. I ignored the tiny, tipped over chairs, the bright plastic blocks and curling paper borders hanging from boards. I shut it all out, scanning the building's foundation, then the roof, for shapes that shouldn't be there.

Ridge exited, giving a curt shake of his head, and my relief and fear mixed into a queasy cocktail.

The building didn't hide a monster. But it didn't house Gabbi, either.

We repeated the pattern, circling counter-clockwise. The open yards between each annex seemed endless, every muscle tensed for something to rush us. Then the hyper-alert sweep, prepared for a monster to crash down on me from the roof or spring from behind a toppled desk and pin Ridge in the too-small rooms.

Finally, with the last trailers cleared, we faced the circular main building, block and brick covered in graffiti. Most of the designs had weathered except for a swath of intense blue and red whorls spelling out the tagger's initials over what had once been the main entrance.

Taking a deep breath of the rust and rot tinted air, I took one side of the double doors, Ridge the other. At his nod, we swept in, guns level. I cringed at the crunch of glass shards under my soles.

We ended with our backs against the walls, beams from the light mounted on our barrels haloing scattered trash, the school's stingray mascot banner hanging from one rivet. More glass from the destroyed safety barriers separating the public entry from the cafeteria winked back from among the litter. And a yawning darkness ahead, our lights not penetrating more than a few feet down the hallway.

Without the breeze, the placed seemed to close in, sweaty-dank air settling on my skin and seeping in. The stench—I resorted to shallows breaths and pulling the balaclava on, the rank ammonia of urine saturating the stale air. It smelled like a giant cat had turned the place into an unemptied litter box.

At the apex of the hall, Ridge held up his fist. The school divided here, a shorter hall on one side, the open cafeteria on the other, then the central hall leading back.

After a second, he pointed left.

I grasped his reasoning. Failing to check the short hall first could leave an enemy at our backs once we ventured further in.

We repeated the clearance sweep, pushing forward in unison. Splitting, slamming our backs to the walls and scanning.

Only a few steps in, the beams from our guns settled on a taller pile of trash, dark paint from another graffiti spree or party spilled around it.

The stink here took on a new, sweet-rotten edge, miasma so strong it felt like it should be visible. This was meat gone bad in the fridge, times a hundred. Or a human-sized body left to rot. Bile and panic scalded up my throat.

Ridge's hand closed over my shoulder, jerking me to a stop. My muscles had taken over, moving without asking my brain first. He caught my gaze and held it, eyes behind his mask steady. The micro time-out let me scratch up a shred of control, remember my training. Think about the two class-room doors between us and the pile, and potential ambushes.

When I nodded, jerky but understandable, he turned loose. I approached the trash that wasn't trash carefully, Ridge scanning further out around us. Clearing each class-room as I stayed by the room's door, watching our backs for traps. Straining to make out details of the body. Praying there were no red and orange strips in the hair, that those weren't Gabbi's favorite cutoffs.

The throat-clogging ripeness of decaying meat intensified with each step. My shoes left clear patches in what I'd assumed was dried paint.

Finally, I knelt over the body, split open, white ribs showing. The light shook, my hands unsteady as I scanned the corpse. My beam wobbled over a stubbled jaw, the barely-there scruff of a teen. I switched to praying this wasn't Liam.

The light cast shadows over an older teen or twenty-something's face. Blood had pooled around him, and sprayed over the walls. A backpack lay open at the end of one hand, spray cans spilled out.

It wasn't any of my kids, but the young tagger hadn't deserved to be torn open when he'd only come out here to paint.

Ridge's attention was on the hall we'd come down, the only exit. But his free hand touched my back in a wordless question.

I rose and shook my head. Only now understanding what we'd left tracks in was dried blood, not paint. Our prints, alongside bits of flesh that had been a person. I turned my back on the death I hadn't been able to prevent. If the ghoul was still here, I was making sure it never left, and no other unsuspecting person suffered this way.

Ridge moved out with me, his jaw set.

After checking that the main area and cafeteria remained clear, we aimed for the double sets of doors in front of us.

This hall was wider, made for older kids and multiple classes passing each other as bells rang. It should've felt less claustrophobic, but now all I saw were dark holes, ambush points the ghoul could leap from.

Every breath sounded like a red cape, an alert and dare challenging the thing to come at us.

Foot by foot, we made it down the hall. Ridge froze, fist up. It took a moment to get past the white noise of blood shushing in my ears, to understand what alerted him. Then the thumps coming from somewhere on our right were all I could hear.

I whirled, my light bouncing off a life-sized stingray

painted on the wall, right above the word *gym*. Its door listed, only part of one set of hinges remaining.

We eased in. Steps too loud on the wooden floor, echoing in the barren space. Bouncing back from empty bleachers and shattered backboards.

The *thud-thump* came again, the huge room seeming to swallow the sound.

Ridge started right, for the stage at the side. This time, I grabbed him, getting his pocket. I stood on my toes and he bent enough I could whisper, "Left. Locker rooms."

More importantly, also the designated safe area, the spot the school built as its panic room in the event of a school shooting.

I lurched ahead. Ridge shoved the barrel of his gun in front of me as a block. When he had my attention, he angled the barrel at the bleachers.

The image of the ghoul perched on top of the dumpster at the warehouse hit me. Ridge scanned the risers for lurking creatures while I took the relative security of the wall. Working our way toward the repetitive crashing noise.

The opening to the lockers only wide enough for one person at a time, Ridge slipped in front of me. This time, concentrating on the tops of the lockers. I kept my gun aimed straight ahead, and kept us from stumbling into benches tossed at all angles, and lockers knocked on their sides in the aisle way.

The room finally widened, the showers an open pit of shadows before us.

The same decaying flesh reek welcomed us. Piles of text-books, all shredded, plus what had to have been towels and uniforms, created a mound.

We'd found the ghoul's nest. And its feeding ground.

The white of bones made a stark marker, shoved into one corner of the showers. Skulls and femurs with gouges from teeth or claws, mostly. Fabric and packs were dropped in another. The only items most homeless owned, and where the damned monster had gotten the clothes it used as camouflage.

The hard thumps—with a metallic edge now that we were closer—came from what looked like a dead-end alcove past the showers and to the right.

I motioned and Ridge leaned so I could whisper again. "The safety room. Short entryway, then the entrance. Once in the locked room, an exit that leads to a tunnel and escape hatch in the parking lot."

If the thing had accidentally locked itself in, I'd find means via Freidricks to blow this whole building up. Failing that, steal the rocket launcher Kane kept in his personal collection, and do it myself.

"You stay low," Ridge murmured.

I felt for the knife hilt rising from my thigh, reassuring myself. "Ready."

We went in barrels first.

The ghoul paced in front of the thick metal door installed to keep a shooter out.

It worked equally well at keeping the ghoul out. The thing was fixated on the metal obstacle. This creature was larger than the ghoul at the warehouse, nearly as wide as the door. Filthy sweatpants were inches too short for its heavy legs.

My pulse jumped.

Then rocketed again, hammering hard enough to muffle the creature as the ghoul paced over a broken phone, the holographic k-pop sticker twinkling at us.

The sticker Gabbi had slapped on the phone as soon as I'd handed her the device.

I took a step before catching myself. But my shoe squeaked against the concrete.

The ghoul whirled, and its slit-pupil eyes fixed on us. Its

roar echoed back from the block walls and metal door. Rattling my bones down to the marrow.

It leaped before the echoes died.

Ridge's shotgun thundered.

The cryptid flung its head side to side. Shaking off the worst of the blast, a ribbon of green-red blood trickling from one eye. The creature pawed at its face.

Ridge and I split, shoving out of the cramped alcove. Retreating into the larger locker room.

The ghoul flashed past, then skidded. It turned its head, attention locking onto me, arms slashing my way. I dropped to my knees, claws whistling over my head.

The shotgun thundered again. The ghoul whipped around, snarling at its tormentor. Now picking Ridge as the greater threat.

My partner was between pairs of lockers and the wall, the space still too tight to draw his machete. Leaving the shotgun his only defensive choice. With me right across from him, the ghoul in-between, and potentially putting me in Ridge's line of fire.

I saw the split-second he decided against taking the shot.

I dropped my shotgun, sling pulling it out of my way. The ghoul's muscles bunched, preparing to launch at Ridge. I jerked out my machete-sized knife and threw myself at the ghoul's back.

Dropping at the last second, I slammed the razor edge against the back of its leg. The impact thrummed down my arm, threatening my grip.

Holding on, I drew it along the freaky diamond-grit hide as I rolled. A gray-skinned foot stomped inches from my head.

A blast rumbled through the room, an explosion like every firework in a Fourth of July display flaming to life at the same time. Sparks showered down on me, blinding me.

Something rammed my side. Squashing me into the cold cinderblocks.

Then was gone, pressure relieved, my ears still ringing.

At a touch on my hip, I jerked upright, frantically blinking away after images, eyes watering. A hand pressed mine and the knife I'd managed to hold onto flat against the floor. The hurried pats along my arms and side continued.

The watery blob towering over me resolved into Ridge. Crouched by me, slapping out sparks on my clothing. His voice was tinny but understandable. "Don't move, Mac. Be still. I need to check out your back."

I could feel my extremities just fine, plus the slimy gunk from the nasty floors, and the sharp scorching of sparks. The numbness from what had to be the ghoul winging me changed to a dull ache from ribs to hip on one side. I twisted out of Ridge's grip, got my heels under me, and scooted to my butt, sitting up.

"Mac."

"I'm fine." I lowered my volume, scrubbing hands against my pants. Which only served to redistribute the gunk, since my pants were equally filthy from rolling around on the floor. "Seriously."

His hand wrapped around my wrist. "The ghoul ran from the incendiary round. I thought it had—"

"Gabbi." My head got back in the game, the glance of the phone case and sticker vivid. I tried shoving up, back scraping against the painted blocks.

Ridge switched his grip, standing and gently hauling me up with him.

I grabbed his arm, surprising him and dragging him stumbling along after me. I went straight for the alcove again, the one that led to the safety room. The cryptid hadn't been locked in it. Which might mean Gabbi was.

I bent and grabbed the crushed phone, glass screen

flaking off in chunks. The sticker was peeling away as well. "This is Gabbi's. Gabbi!" I pressed my face against the dented but intact door. "Are you in there?" I yelled again, voice rising, throat sore.

"If she's in there, she can't hear you." Ridge held his phone in front of my face. A model of the door was pictured on the screen. He flicked, sending the manufacturer's pitch and schematic rolling.

Fuck. The soundproof door only released from the inside, and Gabbi couldn't hear us to know it was safe. If she'd run into the ghoul, barely gotten inside, she could be wounded. Bleeding, and not able to open the door.

I kicked the snot out of it, only getting a dull thud. Then stilled. "Knife, knife…where is it?" I whirled, searching for mine. It had been in my hand in the shower, and I launched that way.

And ran straight into an immovable barrier in the form of Ridge's chest. "Mac. Stop. Breathe. Why do you need the knife?" His hands rested on my shoulders, steadying me more than stopping me.

I took a gulp of oxygen and put enough distance between myself and my emotions to get back into a professional headspace. "The hilt is heavy duty. I can bang on the door and alert whoever is inside."

"They're going to assume it's the ghoul again. I'll call for—backup."

Which might arrive too late. "Give me yours."

A pop marked Ridge pulling his free and handing it over. I closed my eyes, centered the hilt on the metal, and hammered out the code we used to get the occupants of Gabbi's house to open up for a friend. Hopefully, to let her know it was me now, and safe.

I waited, the seconds stretching out in the silence.

Then repeated the pattern, slamming the door hard

enough the impact rattled through me. A match to my heart, ramming against my breast bone. When I paused, it was to more dead silence.

I needed outside help, and tools. Call Kane or go with Ridge's people—who would arrive the quickest? I turned to Ridge. Trusting him, and whatever resources he said he had. "Get your people. Tell them—"

The door creaked open a slit, an eye peering through.

"Gabbi? Liam? Hey, whoever you are, we're friends. Open the door for me? Please. We can help you."

"McKenna?"

There it was. Wavery and thin and more child-like than I'd ever heard it, but Gabbi's voice. "Yes. Gabbi, it's me. Honey, open the door."

"The monster," she whispered.

"It's gone. We took care of it, I swear."

The door creaked, the heavy metal moving in jerky increments. I grabbed, stuffing my fingers in the crack and helping Gabbi haul it wider.

She fell into me, skinny arms viced around my waist. "Shh. It's over. Are you hurt? Let me see?"

"Liam. Help him, McKenna." She let go of me, grabbing my rifle sling and trying to drag me the same way I'd done Ridge.

I let her, hurrying inside the pitch-dark room. A beat later, and Ridge pulled out a real flashlight, halogen banishing the shadows. His beam lit a path for us, resting on a hunched figure by one wall.

Gabbi dropped to her knees beside it. "His arm—I don't know. McKenna, I'll do anything. I swear. This is official and I'm asking for a favor and I'll do or pay whatever you say. Please."

My heart cracking into as many pieces as the stupid phone screen, I knelt by the boy. His face was flushed, lips dry and chapped, circles under his eyes. He cradled his arm against his body. "Hey. It's McKenna. Can I see?"

Liam blinked bloodshot eyes, then whispered, "It hurts."

Ridge joined me, looming over us. The boy twitched, then moaned as his panicky move jostled his arm.

"Easy. This is a friend."

Ridge crouched beside me. "I'm Ridge. Mac lets me tag along and help sometimes."

The boy looked to Gabbi, who chewed her already-shredded lip, and looked to me.

"He's legit. I promise," I said.

Liam gave a jerky head bob. As Ridge laid fingers across Liam's good wrist, checking his pulse, I pulled Gabbi a few steps away. "Talk to me. How do you feel?" I tilted her head toward the light, checking pupils.

"Thirsty. Really thirsty. Hungry and tired. You came. I tried to call but that thing was so fast and I lost my phone and—"

"It's over, okay?" I smoothed matted hair off her face. "How long have you been here?"

"Umm—what day is it?"

The question ground up what was left of my heart. "Thursday. It's Thursday."

"Since Tuesday. Late. What was that thing?"

"A lab animal that escaped." The lie rolled off my tongue. "Can you tell me what happened?"

Her chin lifted, like she thought she was in trouble or needed to defend herself. "I kept looking for Liam. I know you said you would, but I needed to."

Guilt swamped me. A bit more to add to the load at not telling her, of not being faster in finding her and Liam.

She rushed on. "I finally found Craig, and he'd seen Liam at the bar and told him about this private party happening later where the DJ had cancelled and they were looking for a paid replacement musician—"

"And he cut through here on the way."

"Right. And I found him here because that escaped thing had chased him and he hid, but was seeing if it was gone, and then once he was out, saw my calls and called. But it came back and we barely got inside, and there's like, no service in there, and then his phone died. I lost mine." Tears spilled over, running down her face.

Out of all she'd been through, that was the thing that made her cry. I pulled her against my side, hugging her the way I'd always wished someone had with me when I was younger. "I'll get you another. Plus a new sticker."

When I looked over her head, Ridge was watching me. I couldn't decipher his expression.

I shoved that mystery away for later, too, and checked their progress. "Well?"

"Broken ulna, dehydrated, and shocky."

Fumbling one handed, I pulled my phone out. "Ambulance time." He and Gabbi were getting treated ASAP.

"No!" Gabbi jerked free.

"Yes. Chick, you both need fluids, Liam needs x-rays, and a cast at minimum, possibly even surgery."

She retreated to Liam, who was also shaking his head. "They'll send us to foster care or juvie."

"I'll—"

"They'll separate us. And the house, what's going to happen to them? No." Gabbi's hands were in fists, and she'd edged Ridge out, standing guard in front of Liam. I didn't doubt she'd start swinging if anyone came closer.

"Mac, I know a friend who'll help." Ridge gave the kids their space. "They have a pretty comprehensive medical clinic, and what they can't take care of, they have a deal with a hospital for. They also have therapists."

"Cocoon House." The place he'd handed out cards from. "They rarely have openings."

"They will." He turned to check with the pair. "They won't separate you. You also don't have to stay once you're both better, although it is a great place if you want to. They have classes, job connections, all that. They can look out for your friends, too."

Gabbi chewed a ragged, dirty nail and I stopped myself from slapping it away from her mouth. "We've heard about them. Craig's friend went there." She joined Liam, the two falling into a low discussion.

Ridge gave them privacy, coming to stand with me.

"What if this place doesn't have space for them?" I said.

"They will. When I said the director was a friend, it's because she's one of us. She knows about cryptids."

"She's part of your web of secrecy. Send victims there and—"

"And she helps them deal. That's all. We need to get them out of here, and now," he said.

"Will it come back?"

He hesitated, then sighed. "Honestly? I don't know. Ghouls can be territorial but usually only the females and when they have young. Normally, I'd say we were in the clear and no power on earth could get that male back here after being wounded and then hit with that incendiary. However, I've never seen one go after prey like that, not back off and leave for an easier meal."

"They've been in here, with it, for two damn *days*."

Ridge swore and I swiped my screen to life. Gabbi and Liam were leaving this place, right the hell now.

"We'll go." Gabbi's voice, confident and determined, stilled my fingers.

Ridge jumped in, his thumbs flying over the keys on his

screen. "A med van is on the way. Think you can make it outside?" Ridge addressed Liam.

The idea of moving the kid, who looked like he'd fall over any minute, warred with the reason Ridge wanted them moved. This was a dead-end trap if the ghoul returned.

I chose to trust Ridge on this as well. So far, he'd been right, and reliable. He'd more than earned the trust and I couldn't remember the last time that had happened.

It would be so easy to get accustomed to the feeling. And to Ridge.

idge

RIDGE STOOD BACK on the street, letting Mac big-sister all over the two teens in the House's van. The boy, Liam, was already hooked to an I.V., and had that dreamy expression that was part painkiller, and part sheer relief at the absence of pain.

The van had to go back the way he and Mac came in anyway, so they'd caught a ride to where they'd parked. Not that it had taken any persuading to get Mac into the vehicle. He doubted it was intentional, but she'd guarded the kids like one of the giant white dogs Ridge had seen once on a training outing, guarding a flock against coyotes and mountain lions.

Tonight—today, false dawn flirting with the horizon—Mac had saved teens from a different but very real predator.

Earlier, he's second-guessed himself and his decision to include Mac. Lectured himself on the arrogance of not utilizing other agents during the drive to her place. Then on actively putting a civilian in harm's way, possibly in what could turn out to be a confrontation with a cryptid, during the entire patrol.

His fear had been warranted. McKenna had equal measures nearly given him a heart attack, and amazed the hell out of him as she took the ghoul on. Purposely drawing its attention off him, then diving in, coming close to hamstringing the raging cryptid. She'd had his back.

Pride at her performance welled up, as strong as anything he'd felt watching Company cadets master their craft. McKenna had executed the maneuver as if she was one of theirs, with eighteen years of training. No, like he and Mac had trained *together* for eighteen years. They'd anticipated each other's moves, and supported each other.

She'd understood his shorthand, listened when needed without arguing or grandstanding, and brought her own ideas to the mission when she knew more, like with the safe room. He and Mac...they fit. They shouldn't, too different and on opposite sides, but there it was.

The whir of the van's side door closing brought him back to the here and now. Sera, the director, leaned from her seat behind the wheel and spoke via the lowered passenger window. "They'll be in a room in a couple of hours, and you can come by or call any time." She gave a salute and the window rose, vehicle pulling away. Headed for the Company funded halfway house they often used for civilians who'd been involved in cryptid incidents.

While McKenna was busy with the teens, he'd also stepped out of hearing range and called the Cleaners. He wasn't part of a team, but he was hardly the first instructor or HQ agent to end up tangling with a cryptid during an unofficial patrol or day-off activity that turned to a cryptid emergency.

Miguel swore agents were never truly off the clock and "accidentally" ended up in more off duty cryptid encounters than was statistically possible. Of course, Miguel had discovered and contained a firebug, one of the lizard cryptids indigenous to the desert, at Burning Man the year before, so the guy had no room to throw shade.

Mac watched the van until the taillights disappeared, arms crossed. Maybe he was wrong but it looked less like she was angry and more like she was hugging herself.

The urge to replace her hug with his almost overwhelmed him. It was the same over the top instinct as when he'd seen her crumpled against the grimy locker room wall, not moving. He should've at least tracked the ghoul outside and noted which direction it had gone. Not even an army of ghouls could've stopped him from getting hands on her though.

He hadn't been able to draw a real breath until she's scooted upright and growled at him. Then the fist crushing his chest had loosened.

From his cadet days and courses on civilians, he knew they weren't usually as tactile and affectionate as the typical Company member. And sexual harassment—which he'd never been able to wrap his brain around—was a real phenomenon in their world. The last thing he wanted was to cross McKenna's boundaries, even if the sadness he damn well knew he'd glimpsed in her eyes had leaked out, visible on her face now.

Not able to do nothing though, he compromised. He moved up beside her. Since she'd been fine with it before, he laid his hand on top of hers. Intending to give a reassuring squeeze then let go.

Instead, she rolled her wrist, catching his hand and tangling their fingers together.

"Hey, the kids will be fine," he said. "The setup at Cocoon

is amazing, and they'll automatically get counseling. Sera was serious, too. You can visit as often and for as long as you want."

McKenna sighed, the set of her shoulders giving away her weariness. "I don't know what's wrong with me."

"You found out about an unknown threat the hard way, and almost lost people to it."

"I should be over that, not acting like—whatever this is." She glanced at their joined hands, a quick corner of her eye move. "The kids are safe, and I should be working."

She was harder on herself than even their head instructor, who handed out tough lessons because she was responsible for ensuring no cadet failed to pass their training and would die at a cryptid's hands, no team shatter because a member fell. "You have been working non-stop. You set yourself the mission to find Gabbi, and you did. You saved her and Liam. Mac, that's the definition of a win."

"Sometimes it's difficult to tell anymore." She broke contact, rubbing at her eyes. "How do we find that ghoul again?"

"I've already gotten in touch with a friend who specializes in surveillance, and another in tracking." Namely, Miguel searching for reported oddities, everywhere from nine-one-one and animal control calls, to private security cams and social media posts.

McKenna gave him a level look. "If getting that help was as easy as you're implying, you would have done it when we began looking for Gabbi."

"At that point, we weren't sure we were looking for a ghoul so much as for a lost or abducted teen," he hedged. Not exactly a lie.

"Ridge, I am too tired to play this game. What is this favor on my behalf costing you?" She planted herself in front of him, like she thought he might bolt in place of answering.

As what McKenna meant sunk in, the new last thing he wanted was to leave. She was worried that helping her and the kids was putting him under some sort of awful obligation, or in danger.

"Not everyone expects payment for doing the right thing." When she flinched, he could've kicked himself. He caught her hand again. "I mean my friends and contacts are committed to helping. There are no favors owed. They're happy to do what they do. Like I'm happy for this—working with you."

He hadn't exactly planned to add that last bit, but it was true.

"Ridge."

He couldn't tell what her half-exasperated tone meant.

Until she erased the space between them, and hugged him.

A full-on, no holds barred hug. Her arms around him, head on his shoulder. Her heart thumping against his chest.

They were both sweat and dirt crusted, and ghoul scented.

It was still the best damn hug he'd ever gotten. He wrapped Mac up, sharing and giving back the same comfort she gave him. The same as he would with any of his friends, and year-mates.

Except there was more to this embrace than he'd ever felt, even for the year-mates who were his extended family.

He didn't want to let go of Mac.

He definitely wanted more of her full-body, full-heart hugs.

He wanted more of her, period. And he had no clue what that meant. He'd been raised under the understanding that Company and its people were it. All the relationships and emotional ties they would ever need.

But he didn't feel this spark, this longing for more, for

anyone at HQ or any Company agent he'd ever met. When Mac's soft sigh whispered over his neck and she let go, it felt like a layer of his skin was getting peeled away.

She circled around to her Jeep. He followed and climbed in beside her.

They drove in silence, the only intrusions the early morning call of gulls as the sky lightened.

Mac parked beside his Company SUV, killed the engine, and made no move to get out.

Neither did he, afraid of shattering this delicate bubble holding them together inside, the rest of the world on the outside.

He should go. Do his mandatory debrief report. Replace the gear, apologize to Miguel over breakfast, and get some sleep. Instead, he sat in the uneasy electric silence that had the same intensity and potential as the air before a hurricane.

With McKenna on one side, the SUV on the other, he sat between a civilian and Company.

"We are ripe and thoroughly disgusting which should kill even a vulture's appetite, but for some reason, I'm starving." Mac's plain statement held a whole world of subtext. A question.

"I could eat. I always keep a change of clothes in my ride."

"Okay."

He popped the buckle and the seatbelt retracted with a hiss. He unlocked the truck long enough to repeat the squeezing in process and grabbing the small gym bag in the rear, all without taking eyes of her, then followed McKenna inside.

Refusing to examine his choice of breakfast with a civilian over breakfast with his family.

CHAPTER 10

$\mathcal{M}$cKenna

I HAD no idea what I was doing.

That statement applied to every choice I'd made since sitting down with Gabbi over a week before. Now culminating with dragging in a man who could as easily find a safety net for traumatized kids as he could produce a fortune in high-end weaponry and tactical gear at a moment's notice. Then disappear a crime scene, and have access to surveillance I doubted my task force possessed.

Potentially even worse, he made me believe in things like trust. *He* was trusting *me* to keep his secrets.

Increasingly, every time he looked at me with respect and automatically assumed we were equals, I wanted to share with him. I liked spending time with Ridge, and, I liked who I was with him. He reminded me that I did help people.

When he smiled like that grin and dimple were just for me, my thoughts went in a different, less professional direction. The excitement that tingled along my skin every time he touched me didn't dissipate when he stopped. Instead, it built with every gesture as if my body was storing them, piling up a charge.

Now, I had Ridge in what was left of my retreat, my personal space. The one place I'd had to get away from playing a role. He dwarfed the room, my six-person table seeming minuscule beside him.

Grasping for a safer headspace, I blurted, "How do you feel about breakfast tacos?"

"Is that a trick question? They're on a par with cupcakes. Nobody hates breakfast tacos."

"Yes or no on chorizo?"

"See my answer to the previous question. Do you cook?"

"Occasionally, but not today. Is that a deal breaker?" If he wanted anything prepared in my kitchen, he'd be the one tying on an apron.

"Nah."

"You are unnaturally accommodating."

"No, I just know what I like." The heat in his eyes…we both recognized that it had nothing to do with breakfast options.

"Right." I cleared my throat and tried again. "I'll take care of food. The shower is upstairs. Help yourself to towels, shampoo, anything you need."

"Anything, Mac?"

Heat blossomed in a whole-body blush. "Anything upstairs." I put my back to him and buried my face in my phone, ordering for us. I didn't turn until the creak of boots on my stairs stopped, and the bathroom door clicked. A minute later, the patter of my shower carried to me.

Meaning Ridge was nude. In my shower. Feet from my bed.

Instead of tamping down a fire, I'd thrown gas on it,

turning a half-assed blaze into a raging inferno. A wildfire capable of destroying me in the process.

With nothing else to do, and too foul to sit on my furniture, I settled for pacing a circuit around the room.

At a thump suspiciously akin to a gym bag hitting the kitchen floor, I gathered up my nerve and faced my guest. Whatever composure I'd gained died a swift and merciless death. Post-shower Ridge was a shot of sex in a plain gray tee and black basketball shorts, shoulders blocking the view up my staircase, biceps and thick forearms on full display.

How unfair was it that even his legs were hot, muscular and tan?

He swiped a careless hand through his damp hair, that styling short-cut only guys could get away with, and stubble showed in the light. It felt like he'd washed away more than ghoul and grime and what was left revealed was rawer. More real. "What can I do to help, Mac?"

Circling as far around him as my small space permitted, I retreated up the stairs, my reply floating down. "Watch for the delivery person but don't open the door. I'll be quick."

I snatched the first clothes I came to and shut the door behind me.

Ridge had folded his towel and cloth, placing them in the hamper. I stepped under the hot water, considering a cold shower to knock sense into my body. But I wanted the physical reminders of Gabbi and Liam, scared and cornered, gone more. That required body wash and scalding water.

I emerged cleaner, but still conflicted. The me staring from the vanity mirror—I'd grown accustomed to the functional length cut, the monthly red and orange hair coloring, the studs and the forbidding, shuttered-off mask.

For some reason, I wanted a different view. Less mask, more authentic. Being honest, the reason was downstairs in my kitchen. Problem was, I didn't know if there was anything under the mask anymore. And if there was, could her judgment be trusted?

The door chime cut my angst off and brought me down the stairs. I double-checked the delivery app on my phone and the front security camera, then opened the door.

My usual driver balanced on the stoop, bag in hand. "May want to vet this order, Miss C." She thrust it at me.

I opened the bag, a puff of grilled pork and lime escaping. "Yeah, this is mine."

"It was for two orders and you've never ordered more than one." She hopped off the porch like she was too busy to bother with the step.

Ridge propped against the entry wall, hands in his pockets. His shorts rested low, pulled across his stomach and crotch and highlighting interesting territory. "Do you never feed your guests, or do you never have guests?"

"Yes." I pulled out a pair of mismatched but cute plates, the intense primary colors the work of a local women's craft co-op. "Coffee, juice, or water?"

"Water."

I put cups by the plates, and unwrapped our food.

Without asking, Ridge took the full plates to the table, another thing I never did. It was easier to stand at the counter, eat, and go. He also put us side by side, dragging the second chair of my pair from the other end and positioning them together.

"Thanks for making an exception for me," he said.

I took a bite of chorizo, lime crema, and beans to keep from replying.

Ridge didn't push, and didn't demand conversation. He wolfed down his food as quickly as I demolished mine.

Food gone, I didn't know what came next. I traced around the scalloped edge of my plate. "I'll wash the clothes and get them back to you."

"Keep them. Like I said, they suit you."

The simple phrase hit me. There was no reason for Ridge and I to see each other again. He was the cryptid hunter, one who seemed equipped with endless resources and experienced backup.

I was a human task force agent working undercover. One who'd screwed up once in the eyes of both my bosses, and was on the sort of probation that easily might end in either losing my badge or my life. My career was a minefield fraught with obstacles.

It was difficult enough for married agents to keep established relationships going, and that was when their partner knew at least the broad outline of what the agent was working on. Considering dating was impractical. Completely unrealistic.

I collected our few bits of dinnerware, turning the sink on.

"I can wash," Ridge said from behind me.

"I've got it. Go amuse yourself," I muttered. Presumably, somewhere with someone who had the basic social skills and clarity I lacked.

The front door never opened. Even after I compulsively dried and replaced dishes. Out of ways to stall, I left the sink.

Ridge took me literally. As I watched, he ran his hand over my bookshelf unit. Touching the heavy llama figurines serving as bookends. Tilting books to look at their covers.

Picking up one by one the fluffy faux-wool and hand-quilted llama shaped pillows on the loveseat, my only piece of seating. Then exchanging pillows for the afghan tossed over the couch arm. Rubbing each square between his fingers like he'd never felt velvet, cotton, or embroidery.

He looked up and caught me watching.

Whatever my expression was, he replaced the blanket

exactly as he found it. "Shit. Sorry. That was probably rude and invasive."

I couldn't take him looking apologetic or chastened. It was—non-Ridge. I wanted my funny, exuberant Ridge back. For him to keep his contagious optimism and joy.

"I did say amuse yourself." I tilted my head at the room to underscore that I was serious, not critiquing him. "It's fine."

That the sentiment was true surprised me. Having Ridge here unearthed a part of me I'd buried, and yes, the sexual tension on top of that intimacy had me antsy. Ridge's prowling, touching, making himself comfortable though? Instead of triggering my need for privacy, it felt right.

How a six-foot soldier, because I was surer and surer that label fit, eagerly picking up my laptop to get a better look at the *Tacos or Death!* cover case, and turning the fandom water bottle all the way around in order to read the tag line, made me smile was as impossible as cryptids. Yet here I was, both things true.

"You really don't have friends over, huh?"

It took a second to process Ridge's statement and connect the dots in his thought process.

Standing here looking at my home through his eyes—a loveseat for one, no other chairs, no photos, the sparse kitchen, I grasped how he came to his conclusion. Again, instead of feeling violated or defensive, his understanding fed the flame, one completely separate from the pure lust, and located in my chest.

Where the sexual tension felt like an out of control wildfire, the other was a warm campfire, a safe and welcoming place to thaw out. I also owed Ridge an answer. "My life is complicated. On top of that, I prefer to keep my co-workers strictly as co-workers, not friends. They aren't—"

"They aren't your type, or the people you want to spend extra time with. You are a good person." Ridge left my knickknacks and met me. I hadn't taken time to dry my hair, and he caught one of the flyaway strands and curled it around his finger.

My skin felt too tight, shivers racing across it similar to having a fever, although I felt anything but sick as he continued. "You are kind, and smart, and brave. I don't know why you're involved in this career, but I do know you are incredible and way too good for it and those people."

He let the curl he'd formed go and touched my jaw, the compassion in his eyes as clear as a sunny day.

I turned my face into the caress. Taking that as permission, he swept his thumb along the edge of my jaw to my chin, then to my lips. Rough pad of his thumb tracing them and sending a surge of want through me.

He rested his thumb against the center of my lower lip. "You're beautiful, too. Wow, are you beautiful."

"So are you," I whispered. "What's your position on kissing?"

"Enthusiastic." This smile was new, wicked and promising we'd end up naked.

He dug his free hand into my hair, scars and calluses catching and sending micro-currents straight between my legs. He cupped the back of my head. Asking, giving me time and the choice of moving from friends to more.

I followed the light pressure, and wedged in tight against him. Free now to notice the muscles and planes I'd forced myself to ignore during my impulsive hug on the street.

He drew his thumb down my lip, teasing and slow. Drawing the moment out. The instant it cleared my skin, he replaced it with his lips. He still took his time, playing with pressure and angles. In no hurry, acting as if this was the most important task he had all day.

I opened up as his fingers massaged my scalp, mimicking

what his tongue was doing. Playful and hot as hell, so very Ridge.

I rested my hands at his waist, and he pressed into my touch, letting me know he liked the contact. When I rolled the edge of his tee between my fingers, he lifted his lips enough to growl, "Yeah. Touch me anywhere. Amuse yourself all you want." Repeating my offer back to me.

I felt his naughty smile when we resumed our kiss. His ease hit some lock deep inside me. Ridge was the key, and made it okay to play again. To enjoy for the sake of it, not to think about how what I did looked to others, whether it matched the character I was playing, whether it would make the members of the task force discount me as a flaky woman, or make them more suspicious of my motives and loyalties.

I ran both hands under his shirt, palms flat against his stomach. Reacquainting myself with physical contact that didn't involve violence. Enjoying defined muscles used to help others, warm skin, and the way he twitched and leaned harder as my hands traveled over hard abs, up to his chest, mapping the solidness, over to strong shoulders. What felt like a raised scar ran along one.

His tongue explored me with the same fascination, tangling with mine. Flicking along my now sensitive lips, then darting back in.

Ridge kissed the same way he moved through life—skillfully, confident, and paying attention to the other person. That feeling of being the sole focus of his attention, the only thing that mattered to him, wound around that already warm spot in my chest with his name on it. Then twisted lower and I arched against him.

At the answering bulge against my stomach, my fingers dug into his shoulders.

Ridge swore but when I loosened my grip, his hand went

to the small of my back, keeping us pressed tight. "Table, kitchen counter, or upstairs?" He asked.

"Condoms are upstairs."

He shifted enough to grab under my ass, lifting me. I locked my legs around his waist, and my arms around his neck. He climbed the stairs like I didn't weigh as much as his gym bag, never taking lips off mine until we arrived. Then, only to double check. "Bed?"

"Yes." Yes, I wanted him in my bed, and yes, I wanted our clothes gone, no barriers between us.

He knelt and set me on the comforter. Did that thing, brushing fingers along my cheek, feather-light, like I was … maybe not breakable, but important. Precious. "I want to look at you."

I shifted to wiggle out of my tee and yoga pants.

Ridge touched my sleeve, brows up in question.

I let go, and he kissed me, before catching my shirt hem. He bent his head, rolling the fabric inch-by-inch, and kissing as he went.

I gasped, fingers digging into the edge of the mattress at the sensations of soft lips and the bur of day-old stubble. Nipples pebbling like I'd stepped into the ocean in February.

"Arms."

I held mine up, helping Ridge get rid of my shirt. He immediately went back to his work. Catching a nipple, sucking on it through the thin cotton of my bra. His fingers were busy tweaking my other nipple, giving everyone equal attention.

I arched and shoved my breast into his hand. He experimented with how firm, pinching, and I arched into the pressure. Somehow, the front clasp gave and the bra fell. Ridge switched between nipples, tongue circling, hands cupping my breasts.

I shimmied, not able to stay still.

Keeping one hand busy with my aching nipple, he worked his way down, kissing and nibbling. When I moaned and bucked, lifting off the bed, shoving against his lips, he rolled his cheek against me, stubble leaving a trail of goosebumps. Checking with me.

I raised my hips and he worked the leggings off, big hands cupping my thighs, then running down my calves.

He kissed along my inner thighs, switching his attention back and forth. Nipping a line from hipbone to hipbone at the top of my briefs, just above where I wanted his mouth. Repeating the process as he tugged the boycut brief off.

"Fuck but you're pretty all over." The way his gaze feasted on me—

I changed *wanted* to *needed.* "Ridge."

"I've got you." He traced random patterns from my navel down. Fingers dancing and teasing. Swirling along skin already trying to crawl off my body.

Then his head was between my thighs. Kissing where fingers had gone. Stopping over my center, breath brushing over my clit, already wet, and I bucked again.

His tongue took over. Circling in lazy spirals. Close, so close, then away. Teasing. Bringing me close then retreating. The blanket bunched between my fingers. Every part of me vibrating.

Like he knew exactly where my line was, Ridge committed. Finding my clit. Swirling around it, pressure increasing. Turning me into one naked nerve.

I came, white noise momentarily blocking out the world. Riding the waves of pleasure that kept cresting. They quieted, and it took true effort to raise my head.

Ridge still knelt in front of me. Whimsy, but it felt like he was worshipping me.

"Come up here." I curled my fingers in an order-invitation.

He picked me up again and moved us to the center of my bed. Like he couldn't keep from touching, he stroked along my leg, then up. Pausing, he frowned at the bruised that had made an appearance from my shoulder to mid-ribcage, my souvenir from the ghoul knocking me out of its way.

Ridge didn't deserve to be worried. I wanted him to feel as good as I did. I wrapped the drawstring of his shorts around my finger, his erection clearly outlined and telling me he'd gone commando. "I've wanted to see you naked since you showed up in my parking lot." I tugged at the string.

He grabbed the hem of his shirt. I propped up on my elbows for a better view, and coughed.

"You have a request, Cabello?"

I took a go at mimicking his cheekiness. "As a matter of fact, I do. Take your time, please and thank you."

"You want a show?" That grin, devilish as sin despite the dimple, lit him up.

"What would I have to do to get one?"

"All you ever have to do is ask, ma'am."

He backed off the bed, and far enough away that I wasn't craning my neck at impossible angles.

He grabbed the hem of his tee, arms crossed. Muscles in his arms flexed, but he took the shirt off in slow motion, drawing it out. Revealing abs that looked hard enough to rival granite. Then sculpted pecs, and those killer shoulders.

Twirling the shirt, he posed. For real popping one pec, then the other, like he'd spent time in a male stripper troupe. Which should've been silly as hell, but…I sat all the way up.

He stretched the shirt between both hands, and turned. I got my first view of his back. As sculpted as his chest, with what looked like a row of old, white scars between his shoulder blades. He held the shirt over his head, hips moving to music we didn't have. Then tossed the tee backwards at me.

I batted it out of my way.

He eased the shorts lower. Sliding down the curve of his ass, and good Lord. He clenched ass cheeks, and I wished I had a quarter to bounce. Until he jerked them back up. "Not fair, Prescott."

"You'll get your money's worth. Don't you worry." He swiveled his hips and turned. Hooking his thumbs in his waistband, already low enough to follow the cut V, flat muscles tapering and disappearing under the fabric.

He did another flex and shimmy, and changed tactics. Sliding his palms down either side of his erection, leaving no question about size or arousal. Finally he jerked and let the shorts go. Posing in front of me, grabbing the base of his cock and working his hand to the tip.

His body was a work of art, the scars adding to the effect instead of detracting.

I crooked my finger and he stalked over. I touched his hand, trailing my fingers up, hairs crisp under my fingertips. I kissed over the healing lacerations from the first ghoul. Then over the newer abrasions from today. They were the physical proof of his skill and courage.

Marks he'd earned helping me, because for whatever reason, that mattered to him.

I drew from one old scar to another, some white and faded, some pinker lines. Punctures, too. "Turn?"

He obeyed. Letting me do as I would. I ran hands over his shoulders, velvet skin over solid muscles. Down his spine, getting a shiver from him before he caught himself. I drew my short nails over that ass. "This? This is art."

"Condoms, Mac?"

I grinned at the strain in his voice. My breast brushing

over his hip, I bent around him and palmed my nightstand drawer, grabbing a packet.

Ridge poked at the drawer contents, checking out the vibrator and toys on display. "Oh, hell yes. We're playing with these next time."

My breath caught for a second at his casual promise, that he wasn't thinking one and done.

At the rip of foil, Ridge turned, cock ready and eager.

I circled him at the base and he groaned. I rolled the condom on, sliding my hand behind. Backing up, I invited Ridge onto the bed.

He crawled on, knees bumping mine. Caught the back of my neck and kissed me, more tongue and teeth this time.

"Hold on to me," he said, voice a hungry bass growl.

I grabbed his shoulders as he gripped my hips and lifted me onto his cock. Once I was secure, he switched, arm behind my back and the other hand going between our joined bodies. His fingers found my clit.

Firm but gentle, he circled. His hips moving in the same slow, easy rhythm. Never taking his gaze from mine, the same as he'd done when we arrived. Muscles flexing and contracting, arm strong and sure around me. Promising he wouldn't let me fall.

The pressure built again, higher and higher, and he picked up the tempo. The bed shaking against the wall, violent enough if I'd had neighbors at home, they'd have called the police.

My orgasm rolled through me, Ridge's starting as mine mellowed, hips pumping. I clenched around him and his grip tightened. Keeping me close. Staring into each other, too deep. Seeing more than lust, or like, or even friendship.

Despite his hold, I fell. Not physically, but a more dangerous descent than even a dive off a cliff.

I was falling for Ridge Prescott. Except, he didn't really know who the real McKenna Cabello was.

CHAPTER 11

idge

RIDGE HELD ONTO MCKENNA, awed, and honored, and not only by the mind-blowing sex.

Mac had let him in. She'd let him *see* her, no hiding, no sharp defensive edges. She'd allowed him in her space not because she had no choice but because she wanted him here. He recognized how much trust that required on her part.

He kept her close, tucked against his chest, and when she tightened her hold around his neck, buried his face in her fucking amazing bonfire hair. Catching a hit of the same spice and citrus body wash he'd discovered in her shower. That was Mac all over—she was heat and fire and action, not sweet and soothing.

Confusing as hell. He added that to his Everything About McKenna list.

He'd figured out long ago that the civilian world didn't

approach sex the way Company did. Yet another reason no agent he'd ever met had slept with a civi.

For him and every other agent, sex was simple fun. Easy. The only true emotional relationships were between teams. That insularity, that singular focus, was what allowed the Company to exist and carry out their mission. For agents, sex wasn't fraught with power dynamics or entanglements. No weird undercurrents like civis dealt with, because agents were all friends, and sex was another facet of friendship. No ties, or resentments, or possessiveness, just two people who were in the mood, no other implications.

So he was having trouble processing—this. The feelings Mac stirred up in him. For the first time, those feelings were stronger now that they'd had sex.

He wanted more. More playing with her drawer of sex toys. More meals together. More exploring her tiny sanctuary, and its fascinating discoveries. More of hearing her opinions, watching how she took care of the people around her, more of how her brain worked. More of her storming in and kicking ass.

Definitely more holding her.

The fact that he couldn't bring himself to let her go was probably weird as hell. So was how it felt like she was made to fit in his arms, and he was made to hold her.

Thanks to Vee and her sisters, he had more than a passing familiarity with civilian romance flicks. He'd viewed the civi concept of romance and one-true-loves as the same kind of fiction as space aliens. He'd certainly never felt this for anyone Company.

He wanted more than anything to be part of Mac's life and her part of his, and hell if he knew how exactly to make that happen, even assuming Mac was interested. He cleared his suddenly tight throat at the idea of Mac not being interested in seeing him again.

Her grip loosened. Reluctantly, he did the same, enough she could lean back, braced against his arms.

She frowned, and he added wanting to have a part in giving her more reasons to laugh than to be sad. "I have to be getting heavy."

"I'd do this all day, and be content," came out, his mouth failing to check in with his brain first. "Fuck. That probably comes across wrong, too. Is it weird?"

Mac's lips curved a fraction, the equivalent of a full-on smile in anyone else. "I wouldn't say weird per se. How about unique?"

"Yeah?" Only because she was going to break her neck trying to see his face and talk at the same time, he lifted her off, reverently sitting her on the bed they'd torn apart. He disposed of the condom, then settled beside her.

"You are a soldier who tracks and dispatches what anyone else would call monsters. Frequently, judging by these." She traced over a set of punctures along his hip, a windigo getting in a bite while he was still a cadet. "You have a damn extensive and specialized armory. Yet you look like a free-spirited surfer and everyone's hot boy next door daydream."

"Hot, huh?" He liked hearing that from Mac.

"You are well aware you're gorgeous."

He shrugged. "My body does what I need it to."

"You drop everything to help people you barely know. In the kids' case, who you've never met. So yes, you Ridge Prescott are the best kind of conundrum." She hesitated a heartbeat, unremarkable in the average person, but that beat told him she was about to commit to something that scared her. "Against my better judgment, rules, and hard earned experience, I want to continue teasing out all your quirks and why we—click."

He couldn't have contained the smile that busted loose even if he'd wanted to. "Yeah, we click. Like a perfect team."

Holy shit.

That was it. *Mac* was it.

She was his team. He'd never meshed with any Company group, because his was in the civilian world the whole time.

"What is that look about?" She rolled her lip in, chewing at it.

He felt her pulling away. Company was based on trust, and the bond between him and Mac was fragile. She'd said they both had their secrets but teams didn't keep anything from each other, the only way a team could coalesce and work.

"I want to tell you the truth."

Her expression turned warier. "But."

"No buts." He touched her hand. "You're important to me, and I'm going to share so there are no secrets between us."

"Ridge—"

"Do you want to hear?"

Her hand was buried in the twisted blanket. She was clenching so hard tendons stood out. "I should say no. I do want to share, though."

"Just keep an open mind, then I'll answer any questions you have." Under certain circumstances, there were civilians who learned not just about cryptids but about the Company. He was making the call that this was one of them, using the same discretion granted a team C.O.. "Remember when I said there were more of us who took care of cryptids, and passed information on?"

She nodded, and he swept his thumb over her rigid knuckles, doing his best to reassure her. "It isn't random, based on chance. I'm an agent of Company Alpha Cryptid Containment. Specifically, I'm a Southwest Region cadet Instructor."

The last word left his mouth and a weight he'd carried since McKenna stood over him in a dock parking lot lifted.

"We have a main Oversight group, then HQs in in all the U.S. Regions. HQ trains kids—us—more or less from birth. Some of us go into med schools or research or tech, some into positions in the civilian world. Some train as team agents who patrol and contain or eliminate predatory cryptids. Each HQ assigns and supports teams in their Region." He took a deep breath. "Uh, I think that's everything."

"You are military. And government," McKenna whispered.

Shit. He hadn't completely though through the implications of government equaling law enforcement to someone involved in the highly illegal weapons trade. He rushed to reassure her. "I'm not—"

Mac hauled off and shoved him. Hard enough he yelped and grabbed for the mattress to prevent ending sprawled naked on the bedroom floor.

"You *are*. You're government."

"Okay, yes. That part's mostly accurate. But we only police cryptids, not humans. Hear me? Only cryptids." He took her hand, hating he might've screwed up their connection, and hating even more that he'd scared her.

Mac did that *whatever* gesture. "I should have connected the dots earlier. The scrubbed crime scenes, your weapons, the shelter—it is a shelter, right? Gabbi and Liam aren't being shipped off to learn to hunt cryptids." That last was definitely not a question, Mac's eyes narrowed in warning.

"No, nothing like that, I swear. It's a Company half-way house, true. Sera does take in runaways, but it's mostly for cryptid vics. We help them process, get medical treatment, all that. Afterward, we help them get back into the civilian world, because a lot of vics are homeless or in a bad way. Oh, the kids will have to sign a NDA, and the Company keeps an eye on all vics so they don't—"

"Out your group. Understandable." Her eyes did that

narrow, steely thing again. "What happens if they try telling people?"

"Ninety-percent of the vics we rescue are grateful and grasp the importance of what we do and how bad it would be if the information got out. I know you think people deserve to know for their own safety, but there are a lot of us, we're highly organized, and we are good at what we do. Creatures are classified as cryptids for a reason. Not that they're predators, but that they all have that Chameleon Effect I mentioned—they hide or blend in unnaturally well, and have other abilities that could destabilize society. That's a cryptid."

"I'm asking about consequences for children with as-yet-immature reasoning skills, not about animal physiology and taxonomy."

He fucking loved how fierce she was, how her first thought was protecting people. "The Company also helps vics with school, or college and job training, or career services. We can hook people up with great perks. That one percent who still buck are either conspiracy types, although if they think they are actively involved and in on the secret they're usually pretty obliging, or true criminals. Those are turned over to human agencies." And—hell, he'd done it again.

He winced at the we-send-people-like-you-to-jail reiteration. If Miguel wasn't mad at him, Ridge would've dialed, put his friend on speaker, and let him do the coherent, non-threatening explanation Ridge was currently blowing.

Although McKenna didn't even blink at his slip-up. "Gabbi is frighteningly intelligent. I'd love for her and Liam to be in the position to use their brains. And for Liam to develop his musical talent. They're both driven, and work hard." Mac wiggled in front of him, crisscrossing her legs and settling in.

He also loved how she accepted him and his life. Plus, naked Mac was always fucking awesome. "Hit me with your other questions."

"Are you officially what—a branch of Special Forces?"

"We're our own branch. Key officials in all the main government divisions know about us. Like I said, we have Company agents in others. Everywhere, I guess."

"And you are a professor. Of course you are."

He didn't know how to translate the satisfaction in her voice. "Someone has to train cadets."

She rested a hand on his knee. "I should have made that connection, as well. No wonder you're so incredible with people. Your students must idolize you."

Mac's physical blow hadn't really registered but her words nearly laid him out. Her respect came through as loud and direct as with everything she did.

He'd never been ashamed of what he did, but he'd always felt less for not having been part of a team first. Mac though, she admired what he did as much as his cadets admired teams.

It took him two tries to formulate a response, because tackle-hugging her was still way over the line. "They're young. Those aimed at the team track grow up hearing about teams' exploits. I like what I do. I get them the last two years, finesse live drills, build up to joint team missions, get them ready to intern with a Regional team until they're prepared for their own. Pretty sure teaching seems less glamorous than team life though."

Mac huffed, a half-amused, half-jaded blast. "That's the way of the world. I didn't appreciate the skill and dedication my instructors put in, either."

"You had good teachers once? Did you have a favorite track—subject, I mean?" He wanted this back and forth to continue, to hear everything about McKenna. Especially this relaxed, happy version.

Instead, color left her face, and she jerked her hand away, cutting contact.

Whatever he'd said had the opposite effect of what he'd intended. Mac looked ready to bolt naked from her own house to get away from him.

M cKenna

APPARENTLY, incredible sex turned me stupid.

It certainly fried enough IQ points to allow me to violate the first law of undercover work, the rule that kept me alive. The one that had been pounded into me again and again, and ruled my every action for three years. Because I'd just slipped up and all but declared I'd undergone academy training.

Instead of acting as McKenna Cabello, product of the juvenile and prison system, I'd tossed the clues that easily led to McKenna Cabello, college and academy graduate, into a non-task force member's lap. I'd put not only myself, but the other members in danger. I was teetering on the line that meant blowing the entire operation.

My heart did double time. White noise from blood pumped hard enough to whoosh in my ears drowned out whatever Ridge was saying.

Moving slowly, the same way I'd been taught during

courses on hostage negotiations, Ridge's lips kept moving and he held out his hand. The way he'd undoubtedly also learned during his class time.

Tactics he'd mastered in his *academy* courses. Because Ridge wasn't a civilian.

I'd been correct thinking he was a soldier, although nothing I'd ever imagined had readied me for an ultra-secret Special Forces branch of the government.

Secret and *government* being the key words. Track it far enough back, and he and I worked for the same people. We were on the same side.

The after effects from the sick burst of adrenalin remained, but my heart quit trying to explode out.

His targets were different but Ridge understood law enforcement. He intimately understood secrecy and team-work. He'd also had the courage to be honest with me because he wanted a relationship. He'd seen the worst of me yet he still believed I was an inherently good person, and prioritized being with me. Enough he'd shared his secret, trusting my discretion and loyalty.

Ridge wasn't Ryan, and wouldn't bail because he worried more about image than reality.

My panic drained away as quickly as it hit.

I wanted a relationship with this kind, dedicated, sexy, and occasionally unapologetically goofy, person. I'd been messed up by the lack of trust from what should've been my people. I wasn't doing the same to Ridge. He deserved better. Maybe I did, too.

I was telling him who and what I really was.

"Mac, c'mon. Talk to me." Lines cut Ridge's forehead, his concern palpable. "If it's about our being government, I swear I'm not turning you in. If it's something I said bringing up painful memories, I'll shut my big mouth, right now."

"Thank you for sharing with me." I scooted in, rubbing

along his forehead like I could erase the worry lines. "I do trust you, implicitly."

"But."

I smiled at him, borrowing and switching roles from our earlier talk. "No buts. I'm honored that you trust me with such sensitive information. That is an enormous confidence. There's a lot I'd like to tell you, too."

"Is it 'Yo, Ridge, put on some clothes and quit talking'?"

"I'd never tell you that you're prettier when you don't talk, buuut…" I drew the last word out, blatantly looking him and his naked glory up and down.

"Mac." He cocked his head, a chunk of the wariness disappearing. "I think you made a joke."

"Sometimes I get the urge to mix it up." Now that I'd decided, and with that burden of lies gone, I felt giddy. Lighter. I twisted my hair and flipped it over my shoulder, searching for the right words. "I understand the magnitude of what you just offered me."

My phone chirped from my nightstand. "I get holding on to secrets, and acting a part when your job requires it."

My pulse sped up again, mouth going dry. My body so conditioned to playing a role that the truth kicked in my warning system. Technically, Ridge was LEO. However, I hadn't asked Freidricks for permission, and this could jeopardize my career.

The one thing I was a hundred-percent clear on was Ridge never breaking our confidence and putting the sting in danger. "I didn't realize how hard this would be to get out after so long. I'm—"

My phone shrilled. The ugly tune I'd assigned Kane filled the room. He never took waiting well and after the thinly veiled warning the day before, I couldn't afford to ignore the call.

I held up one finger, asking Ridge for patience, leaning over his lap to grab the phone. "Cabello."

"I'm calling a meeting." Kane's well-educated voice was neutral, friendly even.

If you'd spent time in his company, the bland tone sent warning bells ringing. It could as easily mean he'd decided to host one of his notorious yacht parties, or he was pondering ways to disappear your body.

"Among others, I want you in attendance," he continued. "This could be the pivotal moment for your career."

"Yes, sir. The boat or *Sinello*?" I named his club, one of his many means to launder cash from his sales.

"I prefer Sims' place at the docks. I can't call it Sims' anymore though, can I?"

A chill rolled over me, nothing to do with my nudity and everything to do with my body recognizing a threat. "I miss the guy, too. Markie and I both do."

"He certainly thought highly of your potential, and was rarely wrong. I do have some questions before we proceed, and I hope you have the right answers for me. Forty-five minutes, McKenna. Don't be late and miss your opportunity to give me your input on which name will replace Sims' on the company letterhead. I'd hate to think you'd ever bail on me."

"On my way," I said to the dead line, Kane already cutting our connection. Fuck, but he was in a mood.

That the meet wasn't going down at his yacht, his preferred site for disappearing people as well as partying, gave me hope that today was about me running the gauntlet, the last brutal step before accepting the title as his newest general. The office's warehouse was large enough for his circle to all fit, and had guaranteed privacy from bystanders.

"Let me go with you."

I twitched at Ridge's request.

Damn it. I couldn't call Freidricks in front of Ridge, not until Ridge learned what I was. And I didn't have the time to tell him right now.

"Don't play this off, Mac. As soon as that guy mentioned your warehouse, you tensed up. Is this thing you're walking into dangerous?"

"This is my job." Not in the way Ridge imagined, but still true. I'd tell him everything, but not today as I was bolting out the door. I trusted him like I'd never trusted anyone but I also couldn't have him near me and in the middle of what could turn into a beat-down I had to endure to be promoted.

I didn't have much time before reporting to Kane, and I needed all of it to psyche myself up for what I might be on the receiving end of in our warehouse. The beating wasn't intended to sideline an upper-level crew member but occasionally things took on a life of their own. I'd seen broken fingers and a few concussions.

Ridge swore, reading body language, or at least my body language, too well. "Let me go with you. I'll pick a spot where I can at least cover your back. They'll never know I'm there."

He was correct in that part. But I had to alert Freidricks and the squad, my official backup, ASAP. Even if it was only to watch me ritually get the crap beat out of me. Not calling them in risked alienating them even more, plus losing Freidricks' trust.

"Thank you, seriously, but I've got this." I crawled off the bed. Then hit my closet, pulling out the linen pants, bra masquerading as outerwear, and jacket Kane expected of Enforcer Cabello.

"If this guy has something on you, I can help. We have resources. You don't have to live this life." Ridge abandoned the bed, crossing to me in one stride. Passionate and not giving a crap about nudity.

He caught my shoulders, turning me to fully face him, his

sincerity blazing. "We were connecting. I know we were. Don't turn your back on us."

Ridge was made to be a hero. But he couldn't be mine today.

Tossing my clothes to land on the bed, I cupped his face, warmed by his concern and loyalty. I stole a few seconds for myself, running my fingers over his jaw, enjoying the stubble under my fingers. "We'll finish our discussion as soon as I'm done with my business. It may not be until tomorrow evening, but we will. This is me asking for a rain check, redeemable for a date." If things went south, there would be arrests, depositions, and debriefings.

If I wanted to survive to file those reports, see Ridge and have his arms around me again, I had to get to Freidricks, then to Kane's. I let go of Ridge. "You need to go so I can do what I have to. I'll call as soon as I can."

I scooped up the clothes and holster and ducked into my bathroom. When I came out, Ridge was gone.

As I threw the tailored jacket on to hide the holster, and locked the door behind me, I hit my real boss' number, doing my best to set in motion the safeguards that might allow me to keep my promise to Ridge and myself.

idge

RIDGE SAT IN THE SUV, knuckles white where they clenched the wheel.

Something more than business as usual was up with Mac. He'd watched her slip from his McKenna, the real one, to the persona she'd first worn. Before her mask had settled, he'd also seen the flicker of raw worry she'd never shown before, unless it involved her kids, or when she feared he'd been hurt.

Right now, he was betting everything from his favorite surfboard to his favorite rifle that Mac was protecting him. When Mac went into hero mode, she thought of other's well-being, not her own. He loved that about her.

At the same time, it scared the shit out of him, in the same way as her jumping in front of the ghoul to help him had.

She'd been opening up to him before this call that set his

teeth on edge, even hearing it muffled and filtered partially through Mac.

She swore she had this, and he didn't doubt her skills or competency.

She also had jack as far as a partner or team on her side.

His phone shrilled, his personal setting, not the official one signaling an emergency call-out. He hit the connection on the radio. "Yeah?"

Miguel's voice came through the truck speakers. "The tracker shows you're still in downtown. You up for a patrol?"

Fuck. He wanted to try talking it out with Mac. She wasn't stopping to talk though, and this was Miguel offering an olive branch. Ridge sure as hell didn't want to widen the rift between him and his brother. "Hit me."

"There's some chatter from street contacts about a weird animal out your way. One of our regulars was spooked enough to abandon her squat."

Yeah, that sounded serious enough to warrant a check. "Are we putting together a call-out?"

"There's nothing about attacks, and the info is vague. The main Surveillance desk is all over scouting for the ghoul from yesterday but it's barely lunch time on a clear, sunny day so the odds of it being one, or even a rogue windigo, are next to zero. Maybe a chupacabra or firebug wandered in? Thought you might want to burn off some steam checking it out. The forecast says it's offshore winds today, too."

He snorted. His brother knew him too well. Moving always improved his mood. Toss a patrol at him, then sweeten the deal with the possibility of catching some waves after.

They owed it to their contacts to investigate, and make sure nothing lethal was out there. He wasn't risking putting a street person in danger, or losing their trust by ignoring a request. That the damn ghoul was still alive somewhere in his city, made him itch to suit up.

"Put me down for it before anyone else takes it. And thanks."

Computer keys clicked in the background. "Done. Hit me if you find anything legit. Later."

Ridge put the truck in gear. He had his job. Mac had hers.

The difference was that if he found any cause for concern, one call and he'd have people he trusted rolling out to meet him. He didn't have to face alone things that wanted to kill him.

* * *

RIDGE SQUATTED, staring at the bipedal track stamped into the damp soil beside their contact's tent. What was left of the tent, at any rate. The canvas and netting was shredded, long gouges trashing it.

The ghoul had torn apart the site tucked behind a strip of closed businesses. He didn't get it. The creatures never bothered with pointless destruction. They'd steal clothing from fresh cadavers or vics. They'd break up whatever was handy for bedding. That was it.

This thing's behavior made no sense. It was out during the day despite it not being close to starving, judging by the remains he'd seen in its den at the school. It had obviously avoided all the typical sites the Surveillance desk routinely monitored. Then there was its off-the-charts frenzy trying to get to Gabbi and Liam.

He was missing something, a hint or key to the creature's aberrant response. Rising, he turned in a slow circle. Taking the time to let go of what experience told him he should see, and look at what was really there. The closed strip mall in front provided camouflage from the road and the curious, while the wooded area he stood in gave the homeless a more or less secure area to camp.

Nothing new there.

He switched gears, going back to the tent. The thing was toast, even the sleeping bag gutted. A spot of neon pink and green under the batting and nylon caught his eye. He shoved the debris aside.

The remnants of a backpack lay underneath. Feminine hygiene products had been dumped, a few more scattered outside what had been the tent entrance. He faced the direction the contents pointed, heading further into the trees.

Just past where weeds and trees thickened, another object stuck out. Unease settled over him like a damp wrap and he jogged over. He picked up a bottle, wiping the thick, greenish ghoul saliva off and read the label. Vitamins. Gummi vitamins.

The other items could've come from any shelter. He only knew of one place gummi vitamins and cartoon backpacks could've originated.

This was one of the packs Mac gave out to the inhabitants of Gabbi's house. Mac being Mac, she probably handed them out to other teens as well. He parted grass, scanning the ground. Finding another track, headed south.

Ghouls didn't track prey, even when forced to hunt instead of scavenge. They were purely opportunistic or ambush hunters. But the weird behavior, this destroyed site, the ghoul fixated on getting into the safe room after the kids, despite wasting massive amounts of energy, somehow all those facts fit together.

Ridge knelt, absently tracing the outline of the track. The relentless attack. The kids—Mac's kids. This camp and the backpack. Also originating from Mac.

The breakfast he'd shared with Mac only hours before threatened to come back up. The ghoul *was* tracking. It was after the kids, but they were safe at Cocoon House, out of its reach. So it had turned to tracking anything associated with them—like the backpacks. And the source of those backpacks? Mac.

The ghoul was headed south and straight for the docks and warehouse, because that was the nearest location to it that was saturated with Mac's scent.

Mac had left for her warehouse meet. In plain civilian attire, no body armor, and only carrying the useless Glock.

He sprinted for the truck.

CHAPTER 14

McKenna

THE THREE CARS jamming the scant customer parking meant I was stuck parking at the far end, closest to the dumpster. Normally, nothing of note.

Kane was big on symbolism though. His personal car, the perfectly respectable BMW, sat right in front of the business door. The organization's flashy white SUV with gold rims, and a heart's blood red Charger, were parked in a line behind, like guards for a king.

Whereas I was left outside the circle, with the trash.

My phone buzzed again, the third time in as many minutes. I double-checked—Ridge again. Kane had been right that my attention was split earlier, between Gabbi and my enforcer duties. The kids were safe though and I had to sell myself today. I couldn't risk distractions, not in front of Kane and his assembled generals who'd no doubt all ridden in the Escalade both because of lack of parking and as a show of unity. Yet more of Kane's peculiar showmanship.

I'd already alerted Freidricks and he was pulling resources together as fast as he could.

Theoretically, they'd stage out of sight at the far end of the docks, although their ETA might not matter. We hadn't been able to risk permanent surveillance equipment here. I turned my phone off, tucking it into my only semi-functional pocket. I couldn't wear a wire or earpiece. If things went badly, I'd have to rely on the squad arriving in time, and picking up any long-distance audio.

I lined up my priorities. Convince Kane I was committed, focused only on the organization, and valuable enough to have earned my spot as his general. Get through whatever degrading, ritual bs the all-male circle needed to put me through in order to accept me and still remind me of my place. I'd endure whatever they tossed at me as long as it could be stitched up afterward. This was all about not blowing a three-year operation.

Then find Ridge and finish our heart to heart. Warmth hit me mid-chest, suspiciously close to my heart, at even the thought of his quiet strength. Even more so at him watching out for Gabbi and Liam, and at his willingness to back me up today, despite not liking my supposed lifestyle.

I touched the piece under my arm for luck, and let myself into the building.

Kane sat behind Sims' desk, Sims' laptop open. Going by the sound's emanating from the screen, he'd found the guy's porn stash.

Zac and his attitude problem stood at one end of the desk, Kane's personal bodyguard at the other. They watched me in unnerving silence, probably hoping I'd crack before I ever got to go before the generals in the warehouse behind us.

The room picked up the kind of clarity that came moments before a storm.

Kane spoke, attention still on the screen. "You haven't taken over Sims' desk."

"Nothing has been changed since he died, out of respect. He took a chance on me when I was a nobody, and I will always appreciate that. We also weren't sure whose desk that would be," I dared add. I'd never hidden my desire to make it to a coveted general's role, the same as I'd never backed off aiming for enforcer when I first joined as a street soldier. Pretending otherwise would've set off Kane's warning bells.

He also responded better to ambition than modesty.

"Sims was more than the general who'd been with me from the beginning. He was my brother, always understanding my larger plan. Losing him, especially in the manner it happened—that's been a blow to me." He closed the laptop and laced his long fingers together. Still the picture of a wealthy Texas playboy, two-hundred-dollar haircut, careful three day scruff, and summer weight suit.

His frigid gaze pinned me to the spot. "Consider this the final portion of the employee evaluation, McKenna. We discussed your prioritizing Sims' murder in order to assure the security of several pivotal transactions I have on my calendar."

This was it. Time to sell myself or the job went to hell. The Glock nestled against my ribs, far less comforting with three armed assassins staring me down. Despite his education and wealth, Kane hadn't achieved his monopoly on the arms trade in Texas only by charm and an Ivy League MBA degree.

"I respect that it was weird as fuck, and I do understand how it doesn't lend itself to looking good as far as security for the upcoming business meets."

"A guy in some kind of mask, and my COO filled with

bullet holes does bring my security into question. Let's discuss how the for-some-reason delayed police report said the murder weapon was a nine mil." He gave my side a pointed look.

This was feeling less and less like a formality. "We all carry nine mils standard."

"I also find it problematic that Sims was cremated. Some sort of slip-up in paperwork at the morgue."

So that was how Ridge's group hid evidence of evisceration.

Kane's fingers tapped a thoughtful beat on the laptop lid. "I see that was news to you."

"I hadn't heard. That isn't my side of the island." I lifted a shoulder in a what-can-you-do motion. It wasn't, which was a point in my favor. I had no contacts or soldiers there, no one to pull strings at my orders and try to cover up evidence.

"Markie's version still makes no sense, no matter what context I put it in." Kane steepled his fingers, looking at me over them. "Masked guy. Off-duty cop."

"With all respect, Markie's I.Q. is lower than the daily low tide here. He isn't well suited to situations calling for rational decisions or thinking on your feet."

"Fair point." Despite the seeming agreement, Kane's expression didn't lighten.

"I want to be a general. I've never made bones about that." Heart rate picking up, I went there before Kane could. "Why would I kill one of your favorites, a guy who gave me my chance? The one who also would've put in a vote for me when my time came for a promotion, because I am damn good at this, and that day was on the horizon. Sims never had an issue with me, and I've never had an issue with my soldiers or my streets."

"Another fair point. You were Sims' golden girl, and since

women weren't one of his weaknesses, I do believe his admiration was for your aptitude."

"I don't know who or why things went down the way they did that night, but I'm working the streets to find any clue out there."

"You are smart. You're good in a crisis. You keep your people on a short leash, but don't needlessly throw your weight around. You hustle and show initiative. In a nutshell, you're a businesswoman, and I appreciate that professionalism." He dipped into his jacket, and I locked my muscles, fighting not to go for my gun.

Kane brought out his phone, swiping the screen to life. He laid it on the desk, spun it to face me, and motioned me forward. "But then there's this."

I stared at the photo of me and Ridge at the food truck. Hairs lifted on the back of my neck, although the photo was basically innocuous. "In all fairness, this was taken before our talk about my tabling the search for my missing contacts, and I was searching for any gossip about a strange shooter in town at the same time."

"Keep looking."

I swiped. The next shot was Ridge going into my house. I'd been so smug about my ability in keeping the parts of my life separate, positive Kane had left yesterday, long before Ridge arrived. My stomach went into a free-fall, recognizing how screwed I was if whoever Kane had in place spying hadn't left right after getting this shot.

There was little chance Freidricks was in place yet.

My best chance was delaying. Throat tight, I pulled on training and kept my posture relaxed. "That's my boyfriend. He's a regular person, a personal trainer."

"Markie identified your companion as the off duty cop from the night of Sims' death."

"And I am swearing to you that he isn't a cop. You can

check with your people, do a deep dive into his background, whatever. He's just a guy."

"One more photo, McKenna. Please." Kane's tone was all the more disturbing for its normalcy.

I obeyed. Ridge and I were centered perfectly in the shot from the evening before, both of us in full gear, no mistaking the weapons.

Kane stood. Taking his time, neatly rolling the chair to the side. His composure more frightening than if he'd yelled and threatened. "McKenna, that you're sleeping with a rival's enforcer seals the verdict on your case."

"Sir—"

"Do. Not. Insult. Me." His command dropped like dirt on a casket. "Sims dies under mysterious circumstances weeks before one of our biggest deals, this guy was with you, and now you are on *my* streets in hardware I didn't provide."

Zac and the guard's guns were in their hands, aimed at me.

Adrenalin hit in a sick rush, the room shrinking around me and I talked fast. "I realize this looks bad, but he isn't police or another enforcer. He's—"

I felt it. The shift in the air the second Kane decided he was done. He flicked a finger in a lazy motion, his go-to command.

I went for my gun, throwing myself sideways. Praying to land behind my desk.

The door between the warehouse bay and office exploded inward in a shriek of twisted hinges.

Kane ducked and scrambled, catching a foot in the office chair. He hit, then rolled my way, pulling his gun as he did. Coming up against the end of my hiding spot.

His guard went down, clipped by the edge of the door. Zac got his back to the wall, out of attack range.

Every gun in the place aimed at the gapping hole where the door had been.

A form hurtled through. The ghoul leapt, landing on the abandoned desk, laptop popping and caving under its clawed feet.

It snarled, shark-like head swinging. Scenting the air.

Guns popped. Kane and Zac firing at the cryptid. Bullets hit in a hail, opening spots in the wall, none in the creature.

Its roar shook the desk, reverberating off the metal walls. It launched, landing on the unconscious guard. Claws digging in and using him as launching pad, his chest and stomach pulping.

The creature swung, claws flashing. Half of Zac's face and chest disappeared. Blood spattered the invoices and bills. The ghoul dropped its head, giving wet snorts as it sniffed the body.

"The fuck is that thing?" To my right, Kane was on one knee, jerking his small backup piece from his ankle holster, the forty-five emptied and on the ground.

We might as well throw the pistols at the ghoul for the good it would do. Our only chance was trying for the exit to my left. It was sturdier than the interior door, and would take the creature longer to trash.

We could make use of the extra seconds to get to a car. Kane's was closest, but blocked in by the dead guard and Zac's rides. No way to get to their bodies and the keys.

We'd have to run for my Jeep, further out, costing us precious time.

"When I say go, bolt for the front. Keep going to my car. Got it?"

At my whisper, the ghoul's head swung our way and it inhaled. Then snorted, a satisfied, whistling blast. It whirled, facing our hiding place. One clawed hand braced on the ground, it gathered itself, muscles rippling under gray skin.

Coming for us.

The front window shattered. A dull thump sounded under the rain of glass hitting the floor. The ghoul staggered, blood streaming from its jaw.

The front door banged open, hitting and sticking in the cheap laminate wall. Another form surged in. Ridge braced, a red dot appearing over the ghoul's eye.

Ridge squeezed the rifle's trigger. Blood fountained from the cryptid's face, head snapping back like it had been punched.

Its body took a wobbly step closer to me. Then collapsed, chair and papers shivering at the impact.

Kane swore, all composure gone, eyes wild. He hit his ass, gun coming up. Barrel going between me and Ridge.

"Don't!" I yelled. Holding my hand out, trying for his attention.

His gaze landed on Ridge, the stranger. The gun that was useless for a cryptid but would kill a person pointed at Ridge's head.

I fired. Kane jerked, crumpling sideways, his shot going wide. Bullet splintering the corner of my desk.

I shoved up and lurched at Kane. Hitting my knees beside him, knocking his gun away. He was alive, but blood pumped from the wound in his chest.

I jerked on his sleeve, ripping it free and pressed the wad of fabric over the injury.

Ridge swept past me, rifle level. He stopped by the ghoul for a beat before charging into the warehouse it had come from.

He was back as fast as he'd entered, and knelt by me. Catching my shoulder. "Mac?"

"I'm not injured. Kane needs an ambulance."

"I put our med chopper on standby once I realized the

ghoul was after you." He smoothed hair off my face. "It can be here in minutes."

Minutes we didn't have anymore. Freidricks had to be closing in by now, with who knew how much backup. "My—the police are already en route." I put more pressure on the wound. "I called as I left my place, so they're going to be here any second. And we need that ambulance."

"He saw the ghoul. He can't go to a civilian hospital."

"What? No." If Kane disappeared, I was left with dead bodies, no Kane, and worst of all, no case. "If I don't have him—"

Ridge's hand left my face. I looked up into his open, Gulf-blue eyes. The kindest eyes, and the kindest person. He'd gone out of his way to help me, and the kids. Again and again, because I very much doubted his bringing a fortune in weapons, and hunting down a creature at my say-so had been approved by his organization. If authorities saw the ghoul, and took Kane, Ridge's whole organization was compromised. He wouldn't even be involved in today's disaster if he hadn't been with me this morning.

Who knew what his punishment would be for his part in this gory fiasco. All because he'd saved my life. "Can you get him out of here and have the med flight meet you off the docks?"

Ridge glanced at the room and the cryptid.

"If you can trust me, I'll take care of this place," I promised. It was the very least I could do for him.

Ridge cupped my cheek, expression changing in a blink. "I told you that you were a good person." He pulled out his phone, spoke a few words, and pocketed it. "Yeah, I've got Kane."

Ridge hustled outside, then was back. He dropped the giant med kit beside Kane and had a real compression bandage on in seconds.

He scooped the smaller man into a fireman's carry, and held his free hand out to me. "Come with me, Mac. I can protect you from whatever's going to happen with your boss gone."

"Go. I have to get a fire started." I shoved Ridge at the exit. "Now."

I ran for the warehouse. When I came back, loaded with fuel cans used for the forklifts, Ridge was gone. I doused the ghoul with the fuel, splashing the last over the mutilated guards.

Rummaging in my desk for one of Markie's lighters, I then stepped into the doorway. Flicking the lighter, I tossed it at the cryptid, and slammed the door as flames *whoosed* to life.

I retreated to wait for Freidricks, and the fallout.

None of this was Ridge's fault. He wasn't the one who was so busy daydreaming about a relationship that he missed out on what was happening right under his nose—or at least, right across the street.

Kane warned me about being sloppy. Straight to my face. And wow, had I been. Not paying enough attention to spot a tail when I was in my own neighborhood was bad enough. Kane had either used one of his other general's crew, and I hadn't noticed the stranger on my damn streets, or he'd flipped one of my own soldiers or neighbors, which was even worse.

But to think I was invulnerable enough that even after Kane's visit, I'd still had Ridge come to my house, yards away from where Kane had sat, and waltz in and out bristling with weapons, was criminally negligent on my part.

Whoever was positioned to take those shots with a camera could have as easily taken real shots. Ridge could have died from an enemy he'd inherited because of me, without even knowing what happened.

I'd even strolled into this confrontation with Kane assuming it was only for a little rough housing and then my inevitable promotion. I was completely off my game. If the damn ghoul hadn't showed, and Kane had hauled me into a back room, my being compromised could have put the rest of the task force in danger as well.

At the very least, our years of work were now a huge waste.

As smoke billowed out, burning my eyes, and sirens sounded close by, I let the tears fall. Trying to have a real life while working as an agent might theoretically be possible for some people. I wasn't one of them though. Being with Ridge split my focus, and had nearly gotten him killed, not by cryptids but by my enemies and lack of professionalism.

CHAPTER 15

idge

RIDGE STARED at the blinking cursor on his laptop, the device actually perched on his lap for once. He'd forgone his desk or even a corner of Miguel's in favor of the T-shaped hallway junction between the various department wings.

The surgeons would have to pass this way to get to the office wing to give the quickie verbal report on their patient, or even to the cafeteria first to refuel.

Ridge figured he had until Kane got out of surgery and woke, assuming the man survived, to come up with some brilliant way to keep Mac out of whatever prison the Company would arrange to put her in.

He was pushing it to the deadline as far as submitting his debrief report explaining how a routine patrol ended in a dead and unrecovered ghoul, a couple of dead civilians, and his bringing in a wounded civilian criminal.

Oh, and a civilian business that burned to the ground. Miguel had kept real time tabs, texting Ridge.

Mac had burned down her job and let him take her boss, all to aid Ridge.

Pride at her quick thinking, potentially saving the civilian's life, and erasing evidence of the cryptid washed through him. Awe, too, at her sacrifice to help him and the Company. Mac was fucking amazing, he was fucking in love with her, and he had no fucking clue how to turn around and save her.

He scrubbed both hands over his face, ending with grinding the heels of his hands against his gritty eyes. He gave up attempting to calculate how long he'd been up, between the original ghoul hunt and now. Which gave way to thinking about how he'd spent the time he would've been sleeping. He'd never regret the hours in Mac's company or in her bed.

He had to highlight how she'd put her life on the line, working alongside him in killing the first ghoul, then her drive to find and rescue the missing civilian teens. Finally, in protecting the civilian he'd brought in while keeping cryptids from exposure.

Determination renewed, he dropped his hands from his eyes to the keyboard.

Which also gave him a face to face with the audience that had congregated in front of him while he'd had his eyes closed. Over a dozen second year cadets, his new class as of next week, clustered in a semi-circle. All staring expectantly at Ridge.

His second epiphany of the day rocked him. No matter how the teams or kids viewed him, or the loss of a team-family connection, he did love his job. There was nothing better or more fulfilling than helping polish these bright, dedicated teens into the next wave of soldiers putting themselves between cryptids and humans, assuring civilians' safety and happiness.

Even exhausted, his smile was real when he spoke. "Yo, what's up here? You guys can't wait a few more days to hit the training courses and labs?"

"No. I mean, that's going to rock," said their self-appointed spokesperson. Of course it was Aliyah. He'd seen her scores and evals, and watched her grow up. She'd been a leader since she was old enough to string a sentence together. "Is it true about your mission yesterday? And the one before that?"

Fuck, but HQ couldn't have found out about Mac. Not yet. But if it wasn't her, then what? "Help me out here. What about the patrols?"

"That you killed two ghouls single-handed." The lanky kid beside Aliyah jumped in. Another team leader once the group graduated.

"There were two ghouls, but not at the same time. One was half-starved and kinda runty."

"Hunger makes them more aggressive," Aliyah quoted from a beginner text, the first they read as kids.

That wasn't what he'd meant, exactly. "It wasn't single-handed."

"You didn't have a team or Company backup," she countered. Nothing but another agent counted in their eyes.

Until recently, he'd believed the same. Then Mac had hit his life. He gave the cadets another smile to take the sting out. "I gotta get this debrief in. Why don't you check out the addition to the urban landscape course before classes begin? They finished installing yesterday and you'll be the first to break it in."

As if that was an order, they all swung around, sprinting for the advanced training wing and outdoors.

"The next two years with Instructor Prescott are going to

be epic," echoed back to Ridge as the second team leader hurried his group along.

He shook his head and went back to the report that might keep Mac out of prison.

Like his single-minded concentration conjured it, the ghost of Mac's voice tickled at his awareness. Here. In HQ.

His attention snapped to the left, and the hallway that lead to the outer garage bays, those separated from the Company's every day sets. It also led to the visitor's I.D. entrance.

Two of the Office team, the pair who most often liaised with the Company's civilian assets and contacts, strode his way. Flanking Mac.

A flesh and blood, non-spectral, non-sleep deprivation hallucination Mac, the confident cadence of her stride already familiar.

This version was in tailored dress slacks and jacket, her light green shirt the only difference between her outfit and the pair escorting her. Her hair was even different, pulled back and rolled into some kind of low bun at the nape of her neck, the red and orange tips only visible as a frill at the edges of the restrained knot.

He jumped to his feet, then made a hasty grab before the laptop crashed to the floor.

"Ridge, perfect." The senior of the delegates motioned for him. "This saves us sending an aid to track you down."

He abandoned the computer on the chair and fell in behind the trio, since they hadn't slowed their purposeful stride.

With everything in him, he needed to talk to Mac. Who hadn't even looked at him. Talk to her. Touch her. Apologize for destroying her life. Come up with a brilliant plan in the next sixty seconds, as they all stopped at a door near the front of the Office wing. Murrey's, the head of Civilian

Protocol. He was the agent who had every government agency on speed dial, and whose judgment was final.

Fear, the same flavor as when the ghoul turned for Mac in her warehouse, choked him. The junior delegate held open the door and waved them in.

"Sir—" Ridge pushed through the small crowd to stand with Mac and defend her as Murrey rose. He held a hand out.

Not to Ridge or the delegate. To Mac. "Special Agent Cabello."

"Sir." Mac shook the director's hand, then stood at attention, hands folded politely in front of her. Her posture was different, authoritative in a different way, and formal.

"I should apologize for interfering with the task force's operation." Murrey retook his seat. "We try not to throw more speed bumps into civilian investigations when at all feasible."

"The opposite, sir. I should thank you on the task force's behalf for Agent Prescott's timely intervention. Otherwise, we'd be minus our key suspect, as well as myself. Since the FBI, Homeland, and local agency portions of the force will never know of your group or your agent's aid, my thanks will have to stand in."

Murrey watched Mac, while Ridge wrapped his head around the tableau, tired brain processing the conversation.

Mac, his Mac, wasn't a criminal.

"Standing in as well for your supervisor from the ATF," Murrey prompted, gaze intense.

"As well as Agent Freidricks', sir."

Mac was ATF. She *was* one of the good guys. Elation chased out the fear, and his brain got on board like he'd chugged pure caffeine. Mac was also a soldier, and she was safe. He choked down on the highly unprofessional urge to victory-punch the air and cheer.

"I have to say, Agent. This has been an unusual experience," Murrey said.

Mac's brows lifted. "Not to play one-upsmanship sir, but I think my unusual experience trumps yours."

Murrey's laugh crinkled the lines at the corners of his eyes and lips, revealing the real person under the title now that he'd established there was no threat to the Company and his extended family. "You win, Agent. Still, tracking down an introduction via our morgue contact, and convincing her you were legitimate and understood the threat cryptids pose, was a feat. One made even more impressive given the speed."

"I was highly motivated. We were relying on Kane and his network. He was a major player on the West Coast, but more importantly, he was the key to discovering a cell supplying arms and aid to a number of terror groups." Mac's professional mask slipped for a second, and Ridge watched her jaw clench, then relax. "I also needed to be clear on Agent Prescott's role, sir."

"Call me Murrey, Agent."

"Then please feel free to call me McKenna. As for Kane—"

"If he survives, which seems likely as of our latest update, we'll do everything in our power to gain the information your task force was after. We have no desire to see those three years of work wasted. I can't guarantee intel, but if at all possible, I'll find a means to get it to you in a format that leaves no doubt as to authenticity and chain of evidence."

Ridge's head ached from switching between Mac and their director. That, and digesting she'd been undercover for what sounded like years. And that she'd been hella brilliant using his offhand remark about coroners and the first ghoul vic to get inside the Company.

And that half her reason was assuring he wasn't penalized for helping her. She couldn't know that the absolute worst he'd get was a lecture from Oversight, because Company never turned their backs on Company.

Mac nodded at Murrey. "That information would be invaluable. As for Agent Prescott?"

Despite the question, she still didn't look at Ridge.

"Another commendation," Murrey said, turning enough to include Ridge in the conversation and speaking to him. "You can barely carry all that you already have."

"He's one of our best instructors," the senior liaison added.

Ridge didn't know what to do with any of that.

Murrey switched back to Mac. "It truly is too bad you won't receive one for your quick thinking with the ghoul scene."

"I did what I could given the time constraints," Mac dipped her head at the delegates. "I'm sure your group can take it from there as far as what makes it into the lab reports. I believe we discussed an NDA? I have another meeting later tonight with my task force that I can't miss."

"We've begun the process. I'll turn you over to our team." Murrey sat as the advocates filed out with Mac."

He fell in behind again.

"Ridge."

Fuck. He turned back to Murrey. "I'll have the debrief turned in soon, I swear." All he wanted now was to see Mac.

"No one is going to complain, not when you aced such a messy situation. That was A-plus work. I'll let you get back to it." He held out a fist and Ridge tapped knuckles, reminded even Office agents had spent time in the field first.

Ridge didn't *exactly* lunge for the door, but he cringed as the door slammed harder than he'd intended in his haste.

Mac rested against the wall outside the office, no liaisons in sight, looking more like the version he knew. He jerked to a halt, boot soles squeaking, before he plowed into her.

"They left me here while they're checking—I'm not sure what. The psychologist's schedule, maybe," she said getting the question he was about to ask, the two of them still in sync.

"Yeah, Doctor Jill. She's great." He moved beside Mac, his back against the wall, hands in his pockets so he didn't grab and hug her. "This is what you were trying to tell me today, before that call."

This close, he couldn't miss the circles under her eyes, makeup no match for ghoul fights, arson, and government protocols.

"Yesterday. It's well past dawn. Closer to lunch."

He craned and checked the wall clock down the hall. "Okay, yesterday. Why did you do all this? I mean, not the part asking for anything from Kane, that I get, but the thing about my role and asking about my treatment?"

She snorted, one-hundred-percent Mac for the first time today. "Like you weren't thinking of some martyr-hero move to keep me from a prison term. I know how your mind works."

"Yeah, you do." Which was awesome as hell.

"Little did I know my worry was unnecessary, since you're everyone's favorite here. Another thing I should've anticipated and didn't."

"I don't—okay. Why'd you worry so much?" Which was a stand-in for the questions he really wanted to ask, but couldn't in public, during an official appointment and debrief.

Like why was she standing right beside him but it felt like some kind of hologram, her distant and not really here physically? Why she hadn't touched him once yet? Why he was afraid to touch her, a different mask in place now and a strange flatness behind her eyes.

"Agent Cabello? The doctor is ready." The junior liaison stepped partially into the hall, holding a door open.

"I have to go," Mac said.

Ridge pretty much shoved fists through his pockets instead of reaching for Mac as she joined the advocate without another word or backward glance. She disappeared into the therapist's domain.

"We've got it from here." The advocate waved a goodbye. "Your part's over. Go do agent things."

Ridge retreated to his laptop, doing exactly that, highlighting Mac's cooperation, insights, and general brilliance in his report. Writing out the admiration he hadn't been able to give Mac directly.

Seeing the progression of the case and the cause and effect on a page—it was Mac choosing to aid him at her own expense. She might've screwed up her career, especially if Kane didn't make it after all, or did but didn't give them anything actionable.

He hit send, closed the laptop, and hurried back to the main Office wing, feeling like a hamster on a wheel.

At the tide of warm bodies coming his way, he checked the time—dinner break. He'd been at it hours, meaning Mac had been too.

He edged along the wall, out of the flow of traffic.

"Food is the opposite direction, man." Miguel changed directions, walking with Ridge but pointing over his shoulder. "Barbacoa day."

"I'm checking on Mac—Agent Cabello. She was starting the clearance process when I was debriefing. Save us seats and I'll bring her to the cafeteria to experience the awesomeness of barbacoa tacos. Barbacoa, and you." Mac meeting part of his family, and bringing her into his life, with no secrets? That was going to be amazing.

"I have to give you props on that judgment call. Who saw

that coming—the crime boss was an ATF plant?" His brother stopped, forcing dinner stragglers to flow around them. "I should have trusted your instincts. Free pass to replace all my screensavers with those creepy gifs of cats with human lips." He shuddered.

The consequence-free prank offer was their apology shorthand.

"We're good." Ridge had already forgiven Miguel five minutes after the disagreement. Even if he hadn't, Miguel sending the tip that allowed Ridge to get to the warehouse in time bought Miguel a lifetime pass on prank retaliation. "You've gotta meet Mac. I was on my way to see if she needed a break from signing forms, and invite her to dinner with us."

"According to the update I logged in, she finished the process a few minutes ago. It looked like Murrey was having an unofficial convo with her though."

"Even better. Save two seats for us." Ridge restarted his journey.

"Or, we eat, and you call her later or drop by or something, if you wanted to thank her for the over the top props she gave you in her report." Miguel did that thing, like he was feeling Ridge out.

Ridge turned back. "Mac isn't a call later situation. She's a meet my brother and the rest of my family thing. That cool?"

Miguel studied him for a beat, then seemed to make a decision. "I'll save seats, you hustle your ass to catch her."

Ridge held out knuckles for a quick tap, and booked it down the hall.

For the second time that day, he barely missed plowing into her, Mac and the senior delegate clearly heading to the exit. From the way the delegate rolled her lips in to keep from laughing, yeah, he probably looked about as smooth as his cadets had earlier, racing off in excitement.

"If you're done with Agent Cabello, how about we offer

her a meal?" He spoke to the delegate, but all his attention was on Mac.

The advocate must've checked with Mac, since Mac nodded.

"It was a pleasure meeting you," the delegate said, and shook Mac's hand. "Ridge can get you where you need to go, and you have my number."

It wasn't like his offer was a big deal. They did this with official assets—civis that came on board in potentially helpful roles—have them experience the social side of the Company, cement their loyalty to the people and the cause.

He still let the delegate get out of earshot before relaxing, and smiling at Mac. "Sorry you had to wade through paperwork and interviews. How about I make it up to you? I seem to've read somewhere that you are highly pro-taco. My turn to hook you up."

"Red tape is nothing new, and there's quite a bit more waiting for me after I leave here."

"Shit, right. I didn't think about yours with your task force. All the more reason to eat before you tackle that."

"Thank you, but I'm not hungry."

She still hadn't looked at him, and he lost the battle, fingers brushing over her cheek. Reassuring himself she was real, and offering her...whatever she needed. "I get it. You've gotta be exhausted. How about I drive you home? Maybe catch a nap before you start on round two, and I can have someone bring your Jeep over later."

She stiffened and pulled away from his touch. "That isn't a good idea."

Damn it. They were both exhausted, and nothing was coming out of his mouth the way it sounded in his head. "I swear I don't mean nap as in 'Hey, lets have kinky sex on your llama couch.' Just actual sleep. I won't even stay and keep you awake—I'll be your hands-off chauffeur."

Mac finally looked at him. For the first time, it hit him that her puffy eyes and red rims might be from something other than lack of sleep.

"I am tired and don't have the energy to waste dancing around this. There's no reason for you to reciprocate with dinner, drive me anywhere, or us see each other again. This isn't some sort of social visit. I'm here professionally, praying to God I can salvage anything from the complete dumpster fire my operation and career have become in the last twenty-four hours."

He heard the words, but they weren't making sense. His brain fighting to translate, because Mac couldn't be saying what it seemed like he was hearing. "Murrey honors his promises, you have my word on that. And he is proactive. He won't wait and see, he'll be in with your boss—your suspect —as soon as the guy is conscious, and he'll get you that information."

"I hope you're right, because that's all I've got at the moment. A shaky, conditional promise of something that may or may not prove useful, at some as yet to be determined future date."

"You've got me, and by extension, Miguel. My brother, I mean. He's Office, the surveillance contact I sorta told you about, and he'll make sure we stay in the loop."

"I'm sure one of your delegates from today will be in touch if that's ever the case. Do I need an escort out of here or can I turn this in as I leave?" She fingered the guest I.D. clipped to her jacket lapel. No trace of emotion in her voice, the same flatness he'd glimpsed in her eyes.

Something was hella wrong, way more serious than stress and lack of sleep. "Talk to me. You never answered my question. Why were you worried about me? Tell me that wasn't why you came here, too."

"Of course I was concerned. I owed you an immense debt

for Gabbi and Liam. I truly appreciate what you did on their behalf, and I intended to insure you weren't punished for aiding me."

"Mac, we—"

"There is no *we*. You have agents to train, and I have a case to attempt to salvage."

"But after, I—"

"You are an amazing cryptid hunter. However, you are terrible for my career, Prescott. I'm not one of those people willing to sacrifice career goals for a relationship." Mac looked away from him, and held a hand out to an office aid trying to politely squeeze by them to dinner. "Could you show me out?"

Ridge watched Mac turn her back on him without another word or touch, and walk out of his world.

He stopped and used his brain, seeing the entire situation, from a ghoul killing her criminal co-worker and blowing her cover, to her losing an investigation's primary asset. After witnessing what involvement with him had done to her career, she had every right to blame him. She'd picked protecting his secret over her job.

He couldn't imagine losing his career. The term didn't do it justice, because the Company and his Instructor position was the thing that defined him.

But that might be exactly what he'd done to her.

He had to find some way to make this right, even if Mac no longer wanted him in her life.

CHAPTER 16

M cKenna

I SHOULD'VE BEEN DRAWING out this last opportunity and taking in everything Company in what had to be the most unusual and high tech semi-government…campus? Research area? Headquarters? I didn't have a real title for it, since it was an interconnected complex of all of the above, and more.

Instead, I kept my gaze locked straight ahead, the same way I'd managed to survive entering what was essentially Ridge's home, and standing in a room inches away from him. Then walking away.

As we navigated toward the exit, the employee I'd rudely commandeered kept up small talk. She was as friendly and unnaturally cheerful as every other person I'd encountered since basically blackmailing a county coroner. Blackmail getting me access to the ultra-secretive facility masquerading as a series of companies and housing, forming a privately owned research triangle off the island.

"Here we are." My hostess stopped by the enormous glass enclosed section of offices I faintly recognized as the point where I'd entered, hours ago. "You won't have to go through the decontamination process again. Oh, or the blood donation. Your DNA is on file now." She wrinkled her nose like the process of being subjected to multiple checkpoints, blinding UV lights, some sort of clean chamber, and giving a blood and tissue sample to prove I was human was no biggie.

Self-consciously, I touched the oval band-aid covering the tip of my finger, where they'd done the lab work. I unclipped the ID badge and handed it to her. "Thank you."

She smiled, apparently thrilled to be helpful. No wonder Ridge was the way he was. Selfless. Amazing. Perpetually happy.

I removed happy from the list, the expression on his face as I lied and stomped all over his generosity twisting the horrible dark knot I'd been carrying around tighter. I deserved to carry the guilt. I hated hurting him, but the only other option was continuing seeing him, and wait for me to screw up and get one of my fellow agents or Ridge himself killed. I hadn't been raised with a family or with any kind of relationships to use as training and role models—no parents or grandparents or married extended family. I'd never been *taught* how to have a personal relationship, and obviously, that lack wasn't something I could overcome.

Staying away was the only way to protect him, and repay him for protecting me.

"You have Dr. Jill's information, and your Company delegate's number and email, right?" My borrowed guide knocked me out of my pity-loop. "Is there anything else I can do for you?"

There were limits to what even this place could do, and fixing my mistakes was my job, not theirs.

"Thank you, no. I'm done here." I shoved sunglasses on,

and followed the signs out to the correct parking area, then through the maze of access roads.

A cheery super-soldier who looked way too much like Ridge gave me a wave and opened the final gate. I couldn't quite bring myself to return his greeting as I pulled onto the road to the real world, leaving what I was pretty sure was a chunk of my heart behind those rolling gates.

CHAPTER 17

idge

SQUINTING against the sun bouncing off the windows of the clinic and the neighborhood beauty salon he'd learned his lesson about not entering, Ridge checked his phone. Again. The tic had gone past being a simple habit, left *compulsive* in the dust, and zoomed straight into *reflex*, like blinking and breathing. He couldn't not check. As if it mattered, because the screen didn't show a message or call from Mac, same radio silence that had been in effect since the HQ visit.

"My brother, I trust your judgment. You know that. But are you sure this is a good idea?" Too familiar with Ridge's new compulsion, Miguel busted Ridge without ever taking his eyes off the swirling groups of pedestrians. That, and scanning the various store signs, fascinated by the section of Galveston he'd never visited.

"No." By now, Ridge could draw a map of Mac's neighborhood, with his eyes closed.

"What odds of success are you giving this mission?"

"Twenty-five-percent. Best case."

"You don't have to do this." Ridge's brother quit people watching, planting himself in front of Ridge, and blocking Ridge's view around the corner of the street. Not coincidentally, to where Mac, Gabbi, and Liam sat at one of the food truck tables. "We can leave ASAP. Go catch some waves. Or maybe booby trap the shower in the visitor suite before Vee's team gets in tonight. Hell, we could leave the island and hit the desert—I heard there was a rogue windigo sighted. C'mon, you love accidentally blowing up windigos."

He appreciated Miguel's tries at distracting and cheering Ridge up the last few weeks, including voluntarily hunting, especially something as gross as a 'digo. "I hear you. But you are here in the capacity of wingman."

"I don't think wingman means forcing you to finally quit lurking and go talk to someone who trashed your heart."

"Fine, you aren't a wingman. You're moral support. Like a coach. Pep talk me here." He straightened and quit trying to catch a glimpse of Mac. But because he couldn't stand anyone downing Mac, also added, "And I did burn down her career, so, no stones."

"Did, past tense. That's the whole reason you're here." Miguel frowned. "What's the goal again?"

"Good news, then forgiveness, hopefully. Then…dating? Pretty sure having these feelings for one person and only one person, and only wanting to see them, all the time, is dating. Right?"

Miguel looked as confused by the concept as Ridge had by the definition of wingman. Neither were Company concepts. But his brother was still here, shoving Ridge out of the stasis he'd been stuck in, constantly coming up with and discarding plans to make shit up to Mac in a way that meant something to her. Even if she didn't forgive or ever want to see him again, at least he could do that for her.

Time to execute his mission. "I'm going in."

"Good luck, and I'll be in the indie music store I just spotted, so come find me when it's time to celebrate your success. Or get you hella drunk if the plan bombs. Whichever, I am here for it."

Ridge was pretty damn sure that wasn't the definition of a true pep talk, but whatever. As Miguel moved out, Ridge had an unobstructed view of Mac.

She was curled in the chair, one leg tucked under her. Her hair was loose and the colored tips moved, flickering like embers in the breeze that kept Galveston from turning into a sauna. She had the usual wide-legged pants, but a scoopy-necked, sleeveless shirt, graceful arms bare and no jacket and holster in sight. A change, like the oversized sunglasses she seemed to wear constantly now. At least, when outdoors, which was the only chance he had to catch glimpses of her.

Seeing her would never quit stopping him in his tracks, leaving him marveling at…everything about her.

He shoved his phone into his short's pocket and threaded through the crowd, until he was there. Standing at Mac's table.

"Yo. I didn't know you were coming until tomorrow afternoon." Liam waved his neon-green cast at Ridge in greeting. Then yelped and jumped, leaning down to rub the ankle Gabbi must've kicked. "What?"

"You never listen to me, do you? This is girl code." Gabbi dove back into what looked like mango shaved ice in front of her.

At least he wasn't the only one on a woman-he-had-a-thing-for's bad side. Although he couldn't really be sure, since Mac's face was carefully neutral, the glasses hiding her eyes.

Smooth conversationalist he was, he said, "Hey."

"If you're here for Liam, I can go." Mac uncurled.

"No! I mean, no, I'm here for you, so don't go yet. About business," he quickly tacked on. He glanced sideways at the teens.

When they just sat there, demolishing flavored ice and watching like this was a their favorite show, he looked to Mac.

She shrugged. "You can't be naïve enough to believe Gabbi hasn't already learned everything."

"Hey, people gravitate to me. I have the kind of face that invites confidence," the girl said.

"Invites confidences."

"Right. That."

Probably all true. The girl already had her entire household inside Cocoon House, and had become something like the unofficial greeter.

Also, this wasn't going at all the way he'd planned in his head. He reached back without taking his attention off Mac, and snagged a chair. The only spot open was squashed right against hers. Gingerly, he positioned it and sat, trying not to touch and crowd her.

He lowered his voice, now that he was closer. "There's a job offer on the table. Murrey is really impressed with you."

"I still have a job."

"A desk job. Is that really all you want?"

"It's only temporary. Some truths were—massaged, I suppose. Information that proved incredibly valuable turned up as a result," Mac said. "I assume I have Murrey and your friends to thank. My cover is intact and I can be used again."

"Like I said, he was impressed." So was Ridge at her ability to avoid naming names or letting classified information leak. The CIA now had a very much alive Kane. From what Miguel found, the agency had calmly walked into Mac's task force meeting, claimed they'd co-opted her months before on the down-low and not allowed her to clue the task force in. After, they handed Mac's real boss a file containing everything they'd pried out of the arms dealer.

Equally carefully, Ridge said, "I mentioned my group having assets within civilian agencies. They have that position for you, plus you keep doing what you're already doing. It's another layer of protection. Someone will always have your back that way." Him. He wanted to be the one watching her back. Forget her ever again going into life or death situations with a supposed team that left her hanging.

"What is this, Ridge?"

"A job offer. If you're interested, you'll get a call to officially come in and talk." Because on Miguel's advice, Ridge had annoyed the hell out of the senior delegate, leveraging his supposed star commendations to get to come pre-pitch the idea. Have Mac softened up for the official call.

Mac rubbed at her temples like she had a headache. Or he was her headache. "You can't keep doing this."

"What?"

"Being a hero."

"This is just a job offer, from people who see how good you are. Who appreciate you."

"I get that you felt you screwed up my career, and this is you fixing it. However, my career is fine. You aren't responsible. You never were."

"Okay, fine. So then take the job—I've got no part in it, or after." It killed him to say it, but if Mac wasn't comfortable with him, he respected her rules. "You won't have to see me."

"Seriously? The cringe factor here is off the charts." Gabbi shoved her empty cup away. "I can't watch any more of this. Listen up, because I'm going to help you both stop embarrassing yourselves."

"No," Mac said. "You're all of sixteen."

"Do you know anyone else with credentials as solid as ours, as far as supplying you with relationship advice?" Gabbi glared at Mac.

Mac sunk lower in her chair. "Damn it."

She switched her death stare to Ridge.

"Uhh—" He looked to Liam.

"Sorry, but she's right. You've got no game. You should listen."

"You should think about taking notes, too." Miguel, who'd either snuck back, or simply never left after all, chimed in from his spot at Carm's order window.

Gabbi leaned enough to poke Ridge in the chest, and damn, but had she learned that from Mac? Or had Mac learned it from her? "First, you have been *all over* this neighborhood in the last few weeks. Every time we turn around, there's Ridge."

"I thought you liked me."

"We do." Gabbi's poke belied her statement. "But, hello? Do we look stupid to you? You're here constantly, and always, looking for McKenna. You aren't very good at spy stuff."

At Miguel's laugh, Ridge slumped in the chair.

Gabbi turned her attention on Mac. "You have been mopey-mean and way miserable for weeks. It's not a good look."

He tried to turn the conversation. "C'mon, kid. Lay off Mac. She has the right. Her job—"

"Oh, please." Gabbi gave them the most epic eye roll he'd ever witnessed. "She's miserable because of not seeing you. You miss McKenna. McKenna misses you. Do something about it."

The kid hopped up and held out her hand to Mac. "You two are complete drama, and I'm going to need another shaved ice for energy."

"Do they not feed you at the house?" Mac still flipped her phone over and pulled cash out of the case.

"Sorry," she said as the teens abandoned them. "She gets—you know."

Ridge picked at a napkin, shredding bits off. So much for a carefully constructed plan. It was all out there now though. "She's right. I've been finding excuses to be here, hoping to see you. I didn't know what to say or do, to begin to make up for what you gave up to help me. Then the asset thing came up and, it seemed like a good excuse. If you want me to leave and—"

Warm fingers caught his hand. "I have played a role so long, that I've become adept at lying, including to myself. I take full responsibility for my choice with Kane. I don't blame you. I never did, and I shouldn't have said it. It was the only thing I could think of."

"I don't—think of for what? Help me out here." Whatever it was, Mac didn't let go, and he rolled his wrist enough to cup her hand in his.

"You are amazing. Full stop. However, I'm terrible for you, and I'm terrible at relationships. I wasn't paying attention. So, so many times that could've ended badly for you. Kane's men could've shot you. On top of that, I nearly got you demoted or disciplined for defying rules on my behalf," Mac said.

"We, HQ, doesn't do that."

"That isn't the point. I don't know how to be in a relationship, to balance love and stay on top of pretending to be a criminal, not without dropping balls that impact other people." She took her hand back, swiping at her eyes.

She'd said love.

The word resonated through Ridge, like it had found a matching frequency inside him. He'd been right—Mac was his person and his team.

He shoved his chair against hers. "Listen up, because Gabbi isn't the only person around here who teaches. This is Instructor Prescott talking. You are approaching this problem from the wrong perspective. You weren't dealing with your usual mission, but one that introduced elements you'd never encountered and hadn't been trained for. Namely, predatory cryptids, a second mission involving missing kids, and a brand new partner you'd never worked with."

Mac twitched, that microscopic shift you had to know her intimately to catch. The same one as the morning at her house when she'd said she wanted a relationship.

His heart took off on a shot of adrenalin. "Can I?" He touched the corner of her sunglasses.

At her shallow nod, he lifted them, careful not to catch and pull her hair. He folded them and laid them out of the way, as Mac stared down at the table like it held the mysteries of the universe.

Her voice was soft, almost lost under the ambient street noise and conversations. "A lot of people that—that I care about could get hurt if I try this and fail, and it seems selfish of me to indulge what I want over what may really be required."

"The thing is, you didn't fail the first time. You pulled off working under cover for years, with minimal support, and I can't begin to understand how hard that was. You saved Gabbi and Liam. You had a part in ending not one but two ghouls that'd been preying on this town. You helped one organization protect its anonymity, and still got the required information on your target. That's a textbook win, Mac. And if your task force can't recognize that? We can."

Mac didn't raise her head, but she turned toward him, enough to catch him out of the corner of her eye.

Time to sell this. "You said you took responsibility for

your actions and were good with them. This is me taking responsibility for mine, and I'd do it all again in a heartbeat. I'm happy that we met. I'm hella glad we saved kids together. I'm even happier being with you."

"Basically, you're telling me we're better together is what I'm hearing." She finally gave him her full attention, a question and a challenge in those perfect dark eyes.

"Hell, yes. Not being together suuucked."

Mac gave a shaky laugh. "And that's also your defense for your stalkerish behavior?"

Ridge stared for a second. Then the corners of Mac's lips curved up.

He took a stab at doing the narrow-eyed thing. "Are you messing with me?"

"A little, yes. Blame it on this guy I met, who thinks he's funny." Her real smile broke free, and she straightened. "Can I confess something?"

The awful fear that had set up residence in his head packed it in and left. He swept his hand at her in one of those royal-yes-you-may waves. "Proceed."

"I've discovered something even more earth shattering than the existence of freaky-lethal animals and black ops units." Her grin vanished. "As it turns out, I do like cupcakes. The more sprinkles the better. I might even love them."

He caught her and brought her with him as he rose, not able to stand even the few inches of separation. Then double-checked. "Cupcake addiction is a good thing, right?"

Mac laid her hand on his chest, right over his runaway heart, and tilted her face up. He met her, lips on hers, showing her he had an addiction too. One he never wanted to get over.

When Mac's hand clenched, balling up his shirt, he dug his fingers into her hair. He took his lips off hers enough to say, "Let me put this out there—I'd love to be on Team Cabello."

"How about our own joint task force initiative?"

"Team Cabello-Prescott? I can get behind that," he said, sifting ember colored hair through his fingers, loving Mac's shiver.

Even better, when she ran her hands under his shirt, palms skating over his stomach and getting a shiver from him. Her turn to put a promise into the kiss, that they were their own weirdly perfect team.

She let him catch her weight and rose up on her toes. Close enough to whisper against his ear, "I think we should take this elsewhere."

When he glanced around, most of the clinic crowd acted like they hadn't seen or heard squat. The exception being Miguel, Liam, and Gabbi. Carm hung out the order window for a better view while Gabbi gave them a play by play like a sport's announcer.

In hindsight, maybe bringing his brother along hadn't been the wisest decision. Time for a tactical retreat. "Can we go play with your toys? Maybe on those llama pillows?"

Mac grabbed the hem of his shirt and tugged. He let her guide them out of the maze of tables, past Gabbi and her cat-calls, headed home with his new partner.

* * *

Thank you for reading!

Y'all,

If you enjoyed the story, Amazon/Goodreads stars or review comments are *always* much appreciated. They are immensely helpful feedback, allowing me to write more of what you like, less of what you don't. Your reviews also guide new readers to the stories as well, and keep the writing lights on.

ABOUT THE AUTHOR

Janet Walden-West lives in the Southeast with a pack of show dogs, a couple of kids, and a husband who didn't read the fine print. A Weird Dog Show Chick in her downtime, she's also a past Pitch Wars Mentee/Mentor alum, and a Golden Heart® finalist. She writes intersectional sexy-times romance, and boss-girl fantasy heroines.

She is represented by Eva Scalzo of Speilburg Literary Agency.

Visit and sign up for her newsletter to be the first to hear about giveaways, bonus content, and new releases!

https://janetwaldenwest.com

facebook.com/janetwaldenwestauthor

x.com/JanetWaldenWest

instagram.com/janetwaldenwest

amazon.com/Janet-Walden-West/e/B07DD9FN-Q5/ref=dp_byline_cont_ebooks_8

bookbub.com/authors/janet-walden-west

tiktok.com/@janetwaldenwest

ACKNOWLEDGMENTS

A HUGE thank you to BFF/Con Co-conspirator Deb Anderson for listening to me ramble about characters, and saving my butt during a last minute tech crisis. Again.

As always, thanks to my amazeballs critique partners—Jes, Kat, Mud, Cynthia, and Cath (who had no idea what she was getting into when she submitted to TeamSubversive).

My heartfelt gratitude to the incredible Anne Raven at Black Bird Book Covers, as well as to superhumanly patient editor-extraordinaire Jenny Lane.

Thanks to my sis Amy for telling everyone to go by my books.

And thanks to Mr. WW for his keen eye and endless support.